CONVERSATIONS IN SICILY

CONVERSATIONS IN SICILY

Elio Vittorini

Translated, with an introduction
by Alane Salierno Mason

Afterword by Ernest Hemingway

CANONGATE

First published in Great Britain in 2003
by Canongate Books Ltd,
14 High Street, Edinburgh EH1 1TE.
First published in 2000 in North America by
New Directions, New York.

10 9 8 7 6 5 4 3 2 1

The publishers gratefully acknowledge general subsidy from the Scottish
Arts Council towards the Canongate International series.

British Library Cataloguing-in-Publication Data
A catalogue record for this book is available on
request from the British Library

ISBN 1 84195 388 1

Typeset by Palimpsest Book Production Limited,
Polmont, Stirlingshire
Printed and bound by
Creative Print and Design, Ebbw Vale, Wales

www.canongate.net

F 102, 158
£10.38

Introduction

Italo Calvino wrote of *Conversazione in Sicilia* as 'one of the great *unique* books of our literature'. In his monograph on the work of Elio Vittorini, published a year after Vittorini's death in 1966, Calvino went on to describe *Conversazione* as 'a promise that continues to promise, a prophecy that continues to speak to us as prophecy'. He envisioned it as a work of art parallel to Picasso's *Guernica*, 'the book-*Guernica*'.

Vittorini himself, however, saw the aim of the novel as art form in terms of neither painting nor of prophecy, but of music and motion – the opera. As a critic, he thought the novel needed to be brought closer to its origins in poetry, theater and music, to be recovered from a European tradition of 'intellectualism' in which it had developed into a branch of philosophy. Yet to the extent that he achieved such an opera in *Conversazione in Sicilia*, it was not out of a literary theory (which came afterwards). As he explained it some years later in a preface to another novel, *Conversazione* arose both out of his need to be 'the person I had become' and his need 'to say a certain something which, only by saying it in the way that music says things, in the way opera says them, the way poetry says them, could one risk saying them in front of the public, in front of the king, in front of *il duce*, during the reign of fascism in Italy'.

This does not mean that *Conversazione in Sicilia* is more an act of politics than of literature. Vittorini was a man of ideological passions, and his writing was born in political journalism and commentaries on current affairs. Yet he always resisted, even when it was unfashionable to resist, the idea that art is a vehicle for politics; even in 1945, at a high point of his political zeal, he wrote that 'In art, aims do not count . . . nothing new and alive can emerge unless art is pure and simple human discovery . . .' He was a man of conscience, continually revising his ideas about how such a conscience might be expressed in the world. His emphasis was not on the righteous nobility of 'the writer as conscience of the state', as others have had it, but on the faulty, weak, ambivalent, entirely human conscience of the storyteller. The power of *Conversazione in Sicilia* is not that of the writer speaking to us as 'conscience of the world'; it is that of the world – the sensual and suffering, beautiful and wronged world – speaking to the conscience of the narrator.

Vittorini's obsession with conscience did, at times, make him pedantic, especially in works like *Uomine e no* (*Men and Not Men*). But in *Conversazione in Sicilia*, lyric and lesson, the earthly and the abstract, are for the most part held in a tremulous and radiant balance.

*   *   *

Elio Vittorini was born in 1908 in Siracusa, Sicily, the
eldest of four brothers. Like the father of the narrator of *Conversazione*, Vittorini's father worked for
the railway, and throughout his childhood his family
moved around the island. Between thirteen and seventeen, he used his father's free railway passes to run away
from home 'to see the world'. At home he collaborated
with anarchist groups and student protests (he was
frequently suspended from school), corresponded with
writers on politics, and began writing his own political
essays. When he was nineteen, he married and moved
to Venice, where he worked for a construction firm
and began writing stories, criticism and social satire
for numerous newspapers and magazines. In 1929, he
created a stir with an article accusing Italian literature
of 'provincialism'.

He and his young family spent the next several years
in Florence, living with an uncle. Vittorini worked as
an editor for *Solaria* and as a proofreader and type
corrector for the daily paper *La Nazione*, where during
work breaks an elderly typesetter taught him English
using an old copy of *Robinson Crusoe*. He went on to
publish translations of works by Edgar Allan Poe, D.H.
Lawrence, William Faulkner, John Steinbeck, Daniel
Defoe, W. Somerset Maugham, Erskine Caldwell and
others – an occupation which became essential to his
livelihood after lead toxicity and subsequent lung com-
plications forced him to leave his typesetting job. He also

published a collection of short stories, *Piccola borghesia*, and wrote his first novel, *Il garofano rosso* (*The Red Carnation*), some of which saw print in serial instalments but which the fascist censors banned from publication in book form.

Two events of 1936 contributed to the gestation of *Conversazione in Sicilia*, which Vittorini began drafting in the fall of 1937: he was expelled from the Fascist Party for an article supporting the Republicans in the Spanish Civil War and he saw his first opera, a production at La Scala of Verdi's *La traviata*.

Of the effect of the Spanish war on his thinking at the time, he later wrote:

My thoughts came out of my need, just as my need came out of the life I was living then, out of the love I was feeling ever more powerfully for the things of the earth, for men ... for the children who were mine, for children who weren't mine, and for a woman who, unfortunately, wasn't my woman ... *Mas hombre*, I thought. I believed I'd picked up these two Spanish words from the war in Spain, and from nights with my worker friends listening to Radio Madrid, Radio Valencia, Radio Barcelona; and at bottom my thoughts were nothing more than *mas hombre*; nothing other than *mas hombre*, nothing more articulate or rational than *mas hombre*, yet nothing less blaring than *mas hombre*; *mas hombre* was a drum, a cock's crow, it was like tears and like hope. What does *mas hombre* mean? I imagine it means, if the expression exists, 'the more a man', but in my history it exists, certainly it exists in the book which later became *Conversazione* . . .

Of his experience at the opera, he wrote:

In those days there was a special way of going to the opera, with one's heart full of expectation for Teruel, for the battles in the ice fields of the Spanish mountains near Teruel, just as I imagine Verdi's contemporaries were full of the Risorgimento as they listened to so much of his music, just as Verdi himself had been as he composed it. But the opera in itself, with everything surrounding it of the time in which I was watching and listening to it, made me realise that, in its combination of elements, the opera has the potential denied to the novel of expressing grand universal feelings.

Through music, Vittorini went on to reflect, the opera was able to go 'beyond the realistic references of its action to express the meanings that are a larger reality', while the novel, 'such as it is today among the conformists of literary realism, doesn't manage to foster meanings which can transcend the novel's own engagement with a minor reality, without becoming philosophy'.

Striving both to emulate the opera and to rescue words themselves from the lockstep imposed on them by dictatorship, Vittorini's language in *Conversazione in Sicilia* is an antidote to propaganda. Full of echoes and extraordinarily attentive to expressive sounds that are not words, exactly – from the doleful fife of the opening, to the disembodied 'heh's and 'ahem's of the characters, to the mother's 'old tunes without words', sung 'in a half moan, half whistle, and warble all at once' – it is language bearing mysteries. And as in a musical score, or in an opera, expressive sound and motion are connected – the fife begins the 'movement' which is the narrator's journey in Sicily, a journey which is also a conversation.

Thus the extraordinary lyricism of *Conversazione in Sicilia*: a language which like memory is 'twice-real', existing in two worlds at once: both word and music, concrete and intangible, it is the sing-song language of childhood and a melancholy poetry of adulthood, the language both of modernism and of the premodern fable, of the particular and the universal, of fact and significance, reality and the 'something-more' of imagination (a 'larger reality') existing not side by side but simultaneously.

In 1938, Vittorini moved to Milan for an editorial job at the book publisher Bompiani. *Conversazione in Sicilia* was appearing in serial form in *Letteratura*, the work's subtlety apparently escaping the fascist censors. It first appeared in book form in 1941, under the title of an accompanying short story, *Nome e lagrime*, published by Parenti. It sold out immediately and was reprinted by Bompiani a few months later. But *Americana*, the anthology of American short fiction Vittorini edited for Bompiani, was immediately blocked on publication that very same year: the censors demanded the deletion of Vittorini's notes and commentary.

In 1942, he began to collaborate with the anti-fascist front and the Communist Party, working on the clandestine press. He was arrested, and from jail watched the bombing of Milan, which destroyed his house and all his books and manuscripts. After his release from prison, he redoubled his efforts for the Resistance: editing, typesetting and distributing the underground press, gathering and transporting arms and munitions to Partisan fighters, and organising a general strike.

After Liberation in 1945, Vittorini founded *Il Politecnico*, an influential magazine of politics and culture, and continued his editorial work with Bompiani and, later, Einaudi. In 1946 he ran as a Communist Party candidate for the Constitutional Congress, but was reprimanded by the Party for the 'heterodox' content of *Il Politecnico*, and responded in the journal with assertions of the freedom of art. In 1951, he permanently distanced himself from the Communist Party with an article called 'The Lives of the Ex-Communists'. He continued to run for local political offices as a radical socialist both in Sicily and in Milan, but when elected to Milan city council in 1960 he immediately resigned, admitting that he was better suited to being a writer. He wrote many more works of fiction and non-fiction and remained a major figure in Italian culture until his death in 1966; his independence of mind, prone to endless revision of ideas, earning him both admirers and enemies in the charged political climate of the times.

In the ideologically intense atmosphere of post-war Europe, it's possible that Vittorini's masterwork, *Conversazione in Sicilia*, became too strictly associated with the political and historical context in which it was written, and undervalued as one of the century's great, multi-dimensional works of literature. Literary fashion moved away from works that troubled themselves with too much meaning, with a 'larger reality' or the moral dimensions of human aspiration. Yet now that the ideological conflicts surrounding it have less immediacy, we may be better able to see the engine of Vittorini's book, the great wheel of his narrator's voyage and of his own artistic exploration, for what it is: an intense humanism as vital for our time as for his own.

I write 'humanism' despite the (pointless, to my mind) disrepute into which the word has fallen in academic circles. Vittorini's is a humanism deeply connected to the physicality of language, which is also its musicality: language rooted in the body and the emotions, and in an oral and literary tradition. 'I imagine all manuscripts are found in a bottle,' Vittorini wrote in his author's note – *not*, as previously translated, 'all manuscripts come from the same bottle'; *not* language or literature or humanism as enemies of differences and particularities, but language and literature and human sounds and sympathies as the bearers of unexpected messages from survivor to survivor.

Perhaps it's no surprise, then, that *Conversazione in Sicilia* is a translator's novel – written by a translator, appearing now in its second translation into English. The book was recommended to me by Gianni Riotta, a Sicilian journalist and novelist, whom I met on an airport bus. I read and re-read the opening paragraphs now and again over the next several years, before I had learned enough Italian to read the whole book, let alone attempt to translate it. It is only a slight exaggeration to say that, if Vittorini learned English by translating *Robinson Crusoe*, I learned Italian by translating *Conversazione in Sicilia*. I did not know until after I had set out that Vittorini was a translator; nor that he was also a book editor, as I am. The idea of attempting a new translation myself came to me only when, in an attempt to share the book with one of the authors I edit, I found the existing translation, still in print in *The Vittorini Omnibus*. The outline of the story was there, but what I had loved about the original was missing. The lyrical repetitions had been relentlessly disciplined and cut away, and the passionately musical, evocative language recast in sturdy, sensible, mid-century British English. (The better to expunge any disconcerting allusions, the religiously evocative 'living water' became the meaningless 'live water', all manuscripts were seen to 'come from the same bottle', and so on.)

As I tried to retrace the path of Vittorini's incantatory language as best I could, I also tried to follow the literal path of his narrator: on trains from the north of Italy (watching a writer of a computer magazine send wireless emails from a miniature laptop) to Siracusa (accompanied by a hefty couple in matching nylon '*tutti*' or jogging suits) and by car to Vizzini and Grammichele, since the secondary railroad no longer runs into the mountains there. As in the scenes portrayed by the novel sixty years before, oranges were too plentiful and cheap; a roadside vendor, unsmiling, filled a bag for less than fifty cents. The dry ground was strewn with the empty shells of the snails that were once the subsistence of the poor; shells the size of quarters or dimes, delicately colored with pale pinkish gray or brown spiral. In Palermo, a cab driver reminded me that if he missed work due to illness, his family wouldn't eat – another echo of Vittorini's novel. In Grammichele (the narrator's mother's town), in the large piazza in the center of town, a lawyer in his neat gray suit stood discussing local matters with the town's amateur historian, an old man in rumpled wool pants and a simple brown jacket. Accompanied by plenty of non-verbal cues and gestures – evidence, perhaps, of an unseen opera? – the conversation went on and on.

Every translation relies on innumerable judgment calls, but perhaps just a few deserve explanation here. I've made it a priority to try to preserve the lyricism and incantatory repetitions of Vittorini's language, even when they might seem excessive. Where the literal translation of the nicknames of the two who 'stink' on the train would be 'With Moustaches' and 'Without Moustaches', in the folkloric spirit of the book I've opted for the more playful and rhythmic 'Whiskers' and 'Without Whiskers'. Similarly, where the heroic Lombard is conventionally (and rather loftily) 'grand', I've chosen the more down-to-earth 'big', which seems to me better to capture the combination of physical and spiritual qualities in the original. To preserve the color of the original language, I've sometimes opted for literalisms ('cows' instead of 'sluts') over a more pure, but less suggestive, English prose.

There's no really appropriate English word that captures the motionlessness of the Italian *quiete* but, given that there is a critical opposition between the narrator's state of being *quieto* and his being in motion, on a journey – an opposition that is lost in the previous translation of the word as 'quietude' – I fell back on 'calm' as the least of the available evils. Also, Italian bagpipes have little relation to the Scottish kind we envision when we see the word; a Neapolitan or Sicilian *zampogna* is traditionally made of an animal belly with two simple pipes. A couple of proper names (therefore not translated) carry important meanings: 'Ferrauto', the narrator's family name, derives from the word for 'sharp knife'; and 'Acquaviva', the town in which the narrator's mother encountered the vagrant, literally means 'living water' and is echoed in the later use of that term (with explicitly Biblical overtones) by the cloth merchant, Porfirio.

Finally, the title of the novel, translated literally, is singular: 'Conversation in Sicily'. Publisher and translator agreed that the plural simply sounds better in English, while remaining true to the content of the book.

This new translation depended on the inspiration, encouragement and support of the following people and institutions: novelist and journalist Gianni Riotta; Francesco Erspamer, Ruth Ben-Ghiat and Stefano Albertini of the Department of Italian Studies at New York University; my Italian teacher, Marco Praderio, who graciously checked the translation; invaluable allies Eric Darton and Stephen Holmes; Griselda Ohannessian and Barbara Epler of New Directions; the University of North Carolina – Chapel Hill's Class of 1938; my Neapolitan-born grandfather, Giuseppe Raffaello Salierno, who made me look to Italy; and the American Academy in Rome.

Alane Salierno Mason
New York, 2000

Author's Note

To avoid ambiguity or misunderstanding, I warn the reader that, just as the protagonist of these Conversations is not the author, so the Sicily in which his story takes place is Sicily only by chance. I like the sound of the word 'Sicily' better than 'Persia' or 'Venezuela'. As for the rest, I imagine all manuscripts are found in a bottle.

Part One

I

That winter I was in the grip of abstract furies. I won't be more specific, that's not what I've set out to relate. But I have to say that they were abstract, not heroic, not living; in some way they were furies for all doomed humanity. This went on for a long time, and I went around with my head hung low. I saw posters for the newspapers blaring their advertisements and I hung my head; I saw friends for an hour or two without saying a word, and I hung my head; and I had a girlfriend or wife waiting for me, but I didn't say a word even with her, even with her I hung my head. Meanwhile it rained, and days and months passed; I had holes in my shoes and water seeped in, and there was no longer anything but this: rain, massacres in the ad posters for the newspapers, water seeping through the holes in my shoes, mute friends, life in me like a deaf dream, and a hopeless calm.

That was the terrible thing: the calm in the midst of hopelessness. Believing humanity to be doomed and not burning with a fever to do anything about it; wanting to doom myself as an example of it instead. I was agitated

by abstract furies, but they didn't stir my blood, and I
was calm, I desired nothing. It didn't matter to me that
my girlfriend was waiting for me; joining her or not
joining her, or flipping through a dictionary, was all
the same to me; and going out to see friends, or others,
or staying at home, was all the same to me. I was calm.
It was as if I had never had a day of life, never known
what it meant to be happy; as if I had nothing to say, to
affirm or deny, nothing of myself to put into play, and
nothing to listen to; nothing to give and no inclination
to receive; as if I had never in all my years of existence
eaten bread, drunk wine or coffee, never gone to bed
with a woman, never had children, never hit someone,
never believed any of this possible; as if I had never had a
childhood in Sicily among the prickly pears and sulphur,
in the mountains; but inside, I was agitated by abstract
furies, and I thought humanity was doomed, I hung my
head, and it rained, I didn't say a word to my friends,
and water seeped through the holes in my shoes.

II

Then came a letter from my father.
I recognised the handwriting on the envelope and
didn't open it right away, I hesitated in that recognition
which was also to recognise that I had once been a

child, that in some way I had actually had a childhood. I opened the letter and the letter said:

My dear boy,
 You know and all of you know that I have always been a good father, and a good husband to your mother, all in all a good man, but now something's happened to me, and I have left, but you mustn't judge me badly, I am still the same good man that I was, and the same good father to all of you, a good friend to your mother and what's more, I will be a good husband to this – let's put it this way, my new wife with whom I've left. My sons, I am speaking to you without shame, from a man to men, and I'm not asking for your pardon. I know that I haven't done any harm to anyone. Not to you who all left before me and not to your mother who really loses only the annoyance of my company. To be with me or without me is all the same to her; she'll go on whistling and singing in her house. So I'm heading off on my new path without regrets. Don't worry about money or anything else. Your mother won't need anything; every month she'll receive, in full, the railway pension due to me. I'll get by on private lessons – this way I'll also fulfil an old dream of mine which your mother always kept me from fulfilling. But I pray you, now that your mother is alone, go to visit her once in a while. Silvestro, you were fifteen when

8

you left us and since then, bye-bye, you haven't shown your face again. Instead of sending her the usual greeting card for her name day on December 8, why don't you take the train down there and pay her a visit? I embrace you together with your dear wife and children, believe me, your most affectionate father,

Constantino

The letter came from Venice, and I realised that he had written to all five of us, his sons spread around the world, in exactly the same words, as if distributing a circular. It was extraordinary: and I released my grip on the letter, remembering my father, his face, his voice, his blue eyes and his way of doing things, and for a moment I found myself a boy again, applauding him while he recited *Macbeth* for the railway workers of the whole line from San Cataldo to Racalmuto in the waiting room of a little railway station.

I recognised him and that I once was a child, and I thought of Sicily, the mountains there. But memory opened in me only for this: remembering him and finding myself a boy again applauding him, him and his red costume in *Macbeth*, his voice, his blue eyes; as if now once again he stood reciting on a stage called Venice and once again it were a matter of applauding him. So memory opened in me only for this, and then it snapped shut again, and I was as calm in my hope- lessness as if I had never had fifteen years of childhood, and of Sicily, prickly pears, sulphur, *Macbeth*, in the mountains. Another fifteen years had passed, more than six hundred miles from there, from Sicily and from childhood, and I was almost thirty, and it was as if I had never had any of it, not the first fifteen years, nor the second, as if I'd never eaten bread, hadn't enriched myself with various other things, tastes or feelings, in such a long time that it was as if I'd never been alive; as if I were empty, and so I was; as if I were empty, thinking humanity doomed, and calm in my hopelessness.

I no longer wanted to look my girlfriend in the eye. I flipped through the pages of the dictionary, which was the only book I was still able to read, and inside I began to feel a moan as if a doleful fife were playing. I went to work every morning – I worked as a linotype-typographer – I put in seven hours of linotype a day, in the greasy heat of hot lead, under a visor to protect my eyes, and a fife played in me and stirred mice in me, mice which were not memories, exactly.

They were only mice, dark, formless, three hundred and sixty-five and three hundred and sixty-five dark mice of my years, but only of my years in Sicily, in the mountains, and I felt them stir in me, mice and more mice until they were fifteen times three hundred and sixty-five, and the fife played inside me, and in this way a dark homesickness came over me as if I wanted to have my childhood in me again. I picked up and put down my father's letter and looked at the calendar; it was the sixth of December, I should have written the usual card to my mother in time for the eighth, it was unconscionable for me to forget now that my mother was alone in the house.

And so I wrote the card and put it in my pocket; it was Saturday at the end of the bi-weekly pay period and I picked up my pay. I went to the train station to post the card, passing in front of the entrance, which was full of light, and outside it was raining, water was seeping into my shoes. I went up the stairs of the entrance, in the light; it was all the same to me whether I continued in the rain towards home or went up those stairs, so I went on up, in the light, and saw two posters. One was an ad for a newspaper, blaring new massacres, the other was for the tourism board: Visit Sicily, 15 per cent off from December to June, 250 lire for Siracusa Round-Trip, Third Class.

I found myself then facing two paths for a moment – one turning back home, into the abstraction of those massacred crowds, into the same calm, the same hopelessness; the other turning back to Sicily, to the mountains, into the lament of the fife that was playing inside me; into something which might not be as dark a calm and as deaf a hopelessness. To me it was still all the same whether I took one path or the other, humanity was doomed either way, and I found out there was a train leaving for the South in ten minutes, at seven o'clock.

The fife played shrilly in me and it was all the same to me whether I left or not. I asked for a ticket, 250 lire, and had 100 lire of my bi-weekly pay left in my pocket. I went into the station, among the lights and the tall engines and the shouting porters, and began a long nocturnal journey which for me was the same as being at home, at my table flipping through the pages of the dictionary, or in bed with my wife-girlfriend.

III

In Florence, around midnight, I changed trains, around six the next morning I changed again, and around midday I reached Naples, where it was not raining and where I wired 50 lire to my wife.

My message said: Back Thursday.

Then I was on the train for Calabria. Again it began to rain, to be night, and I remembered the route and myself as a child running away from home and from Sicily, journeying back and forth through that countryside of smoke and tunnels, and the wordless whistles of a train stopped, at night, at the mouth of a tunnel through a mountain, alongside the ocean, in towns with the names of ancient dreams: Amante'a, Marate'a, Gioia Tauro. And so, all of a sudden, a mouse was no longer a mouse in me but a smell, a taste, a sky, and for a second the fife played melodiously, no longer doleful. I fell asleep, woke again and fell back to sleep, woke again, and at last I was aboard the ferry for Sicily.

The sea was black and wintry, and standing on the high deck, that plateau, again I remembered being a boy, feeling the wind, devouring the sea towards one or the other of the two coasts with their ruins, the towns and villages heaped at the foot of each coast in the rainy morning. It was cold and I remembered being a boy, cold yet staying stubbornly out in the wind on the high deck jutting out over the current and the sea.

On the rest of the boat, one couldn't walk around, it was so full of little Sicilians travelling third class, hungry and gentle in their being cold, without overcoats, their hands in their trousers pockets, the collars of their jackets turned up. In Villa San Giovanni I had bought something to eat, bread and cheese, and I was eating it on the deck (bread, raw air, cheese) with gusto and appetite because in that cheese I recognised the ancient flavours of my mountains, and even their smells, their herds of goats, and their wormwood smoke. The little Sicilians, their shoulders bent into the wind and hands in their pockets, looked at me as I ate, their faces dark, but gentle, with four days' growth of beard. They were workers, day labourers in the orange orchards, and railway men wearing the red-striped grey hats of the work teams. I smiled at them as I ate and they looked at me without smiling.

'There's no cheese like ours,' I said.

No one responded, but everyone looked at me, the women of voluminous femininity seated on large sacks of goods, the small men standing as if scorched by the wind, hands in their pockets. And I said again:

'There's no cheese like ours.'

I was suddenly enthusiastic about something, this cheese, tasting it in my mouth along with the bread and the strong sea air, the taste bland but sour, and ancient, with grains of pepper like sudden grains of fire in the mouth.

'There's no cheese like ours,' I said for the third time.

Then one of the Sicilians, the smallest and most gentle, the most windburned, the one with the darkest face, asked me, 'Are you Sicilian?'

'Yes, why wouldn't I be?' I answered.

The man shrugged his shoulders and didn't say more. He had a sort of child seated on a sack at his feet, and he bent over her, and out of his pocket came a great red hand which touched her as if caressing her and at the same time adjusted her shawl to keep her warm.

From something in that gesture I saw that the child was not his daughter but his wife. Meanwhile Messina grew closer, no longer a heap of ruins on the rim of the sea but houses and crowds and white trams and rows of blackened cars in the railway yards. It was a rainy morning but the rain had stopped. Everything was wet on the high deck, the wind blew wetly and the boats whistled wetly, and on land the locomotives whistled as if echoing the whistles from the water, but it wasn't raining, and on the other side of the smokestack suddenly one saw in the middle of the winter sea the very tall tower of the lighthouse, pointing to Villa San Giovanni.

'There's no cheese like ours,' I said.

All the Sicilians who were standing had turned towards the railing of the bridge to look at the city, and even the women sitting on the sacks had turned their heads to look. But no one moved towards the lower deck to prepare to disembark; there was still time! I remembered very well that from the lighthouse to the landing would take at least fifteen minutes more.

'There's no cheese like ours,' I said.

Meanwhile I finished eating, and the man with the child-wife once again bent over her, or rather kneeled. He had a basket at his feet, and as she watched he began to do something with the basket. The basket was covered with a piece of oilcloth sewn at the edges with twine, and slowly, slowly he undid a bit of the twine, hid his hand under the cloth, and brought forth an orange.

It was not very large, nor did it look very good, its colour was weak, but it was an orange, and silently, without getting up from his knees, he offered it to his child-wife. The child looked at me, I could see her eyes inside the hood of her shawl, and then I saw her shake her head.

The little Sicilian looked desperate, and he remained kneeling, one hand in his pocket, the orange in the other. He stood up and stayed that way, with the wind batting the soft visor of his cap against his nose, the orange in his hand, a little person without an overcoat, scorched by the cold, and desperate; while at the prow, in the rainy morning, the sea and the city passed below us.

'Messina,' a woman said dolefully, and it was a word said without reason, only as a kind of complaint, and I watched the little Sicilian with the child-wife desperately peel the orange, and eat it desperately, angrily, in a frenzy, without even wanting it and without chewing, swallowing as if cursing, his fingers wet with the juice of the orange in the cold, his body a little bent into the wind, the soft visor of his cap batting against his nose.

'A Sicilian never eats in the morning,' he said suddenly.

He added, 'Are you American?'

He spoke with desperation yet with gentleness, as he had remained gentle even in his desperate peeling of the orange and desperate eating of it. The last three words he said excitedly, in a tone of strident tension as if it were somehow essential to him, for his peace of mind, to know that I was American.

'Yes,' I said. 'I'm American. I've been an American for the last fifteen years.'

IV

It was raining on the wharf of the Maritime Station where the little train I would be taking was waiting.

Of the crowd of Sicilians getting off the ferry, one group departed, hands in pockets, the collars of their jackets turned up, crossing the esplanade in the rain; the rest stayed standing immobile under the station awning, with their women and sacks and baskets, just as they had stood a short time before on board the ferry.

The train waited for the carriages that had crossed over on the boat to be attached, and this manoeuvre took a long time; and I found myself again near the little Sicilian with the child-wife who was once again seated on the sack at his feet.

This time he smiled when he saw me, even though he was desperate, with his hands in his pockets, in the cold, in the wind, but his mouth smiled under the cloth visor that covered half his face.

'I have cousins in America,' he said. 'An uncle and some cousins.'

'Oh, I see,' I said. 'Where are they, in New York or in Argentina?'

'I don't know,' he answered. 'Maybe in New York. Maybe in Argentina. In America.'

He added, 'Where are you from?'

'Me?' I said, 'I was born in Siracusa . . .'

And he said, 'No . . . Where are you from in America?'

'From . . . from New York,' I said.

We were silent for a moment, me in my lie, looking at him, and him looking at me from eyes hidden under the visor of his cap.

Then, almost tenderly, he asked: 'How are things in New York? Good?'

'One doesn't get rich,' I responded.

'So what?' he said. 'You can do well without getting rich. In fact it's better that way . . .'

'Who knows,' I said. 'There's unemployment there too.'

'So what?' he said. 'It's not always unemployment that does the damage . . . It's not that. I'm not unemployed.'

He pointed to the other little Sicilians around him.

'None of us is unemployed. We work, in the orchards . . . We work.'

He stopped, then in a low voice added: 'You're coming back because of unemployment?'

'No,' I said. 'I'm just back for a few days.'

'There you go,' he said. 'And you eat in the morning . . . A Sicilian never eats in the morning. Does everyone in America eat in the morning?'

I could have told him no, that sometimes even I didn't eat in the morning, and that I knew many people who didn't eat perhaps more than once a day, and that all over the world it was the same, et cetera, but I couldn't speak ill to him of an America where I had never been and which, after all, wasn't even America, was nothing real, concrete, but his idea of the reign of heaven on earth. I couldn't do it; it wouldn't have been right.

'I think so,' I answered. 'One way or another . . .'

'And at midday?' he asked then. 'Does everyone eat at midday, in America?'

'I think so,' I said. 'One way or another . . .'

'And in the evening?' he asked. 'Does everyone eat in the evening, in America?'

'I think so,' I said. 'Well or poorly . . .'

'Bread?' he asked. 'Bread and cheese? Bread and vegetables? Bread and meat?'

He was talking to me so hopefully I could no longer say no to him.

'Yes,' I said. 'Bread and other things.'

The little Sicilian remained silent in his hope for a while, then he looked at his child-wife sitting immobile, dark, all closed in on herself, on the sack at his feet and he became desperate, and desperately, as on board the boat, he bent over and undid a bit of the twine of the basket, pulled out an orange, and desperately offered it to her; again he bent towards his wife on bended knee, and after her wordless refusal was desperately discouraged with the orange in hand, and began to peel it for himself, to eat it himself, swallowing as if swallowing curses.

'We eat them in a salad,' I said, 'here at home.'

'In America?' the Sicilian asked.

'No,' I said, 'here, at home.'

'Here?' the Sicilian asked. 'In a salad with oil?'

'Yes, with oil,' I said. 'And a clove of garlic, and salt . . .'

'With bread?' said the Sicilian.

'Sure,' I answered. 'With bread. Fifteen years ago, when I was a boy, that's what we ate all the time.'

'Oh, that's what you ate?' the Sicilian said. 'You were well off even then?'

'More or less,' I answered. 'Haven't you ever eaten oranges in a salad?'

'Yes, sometimes,' the Sicilian said. 'But we don't always have oil.'

'Of course,' I said. 'The harvest isn't always good . . . Oil can be expensive.'

'And we don't always have bread,' said the Sicilian. 'If we don't sell our oranges there's no bread. And then we have to eat the oranges . . . Like this, you see?'

And desperately he ate his orange, bathing his fingers in the juice of the orange in the cold, looking down at his feet at the child-wife who didn't want any oranges.

'But they're very nutritious,' I said. 'Can you sell me one?'

The little Sicilian finished swallowing, and wiped his hands on his jacket.

'Really?' he exclaimed. And he bent over his basket, dug inside, under the cloth, and pulled out four, five, six oranges.

'But why so many?' I asked. 'Is it that difficult to sell oranges?'

'They don't sell,' he said. 'No one wants them.'

The train was now ready, lengthened with the carriages that had come over the sea.

'They don't want them abroad,' the little Sicilian continued. 'As if they were poisoned. Our oranges. And the boss pays us this way, in oranges . . . And we don't know what to do. No one wants them. We come to Messina, on foot, and no one wants them . . . We go to see if they want them in Reggio, in Villa San Giovanni, and they don't want them . . . No one wants them.'

The engineer's horn sounded, the train whistled.

'No one wants them . . . We go back and forth, we have to pay for the trip for us and for them, too, we don't eat any bread, but no one wants them . . . No one wants them.'

The train was moving, I jumped to a door.

'Goodbye, goodbye!'

'No one wants them . . . No one wants them . . . As if they were poisoned . . . Damned oranges!'

V

I had hardly thrown myself onto the wooden seat, the train in motion, when I heard two voices in the corridor, talking to each other about the incident.

Nothing had happened, nothing that was a real incident, nor a fact, nor even a gesture; only that a man, that little Sicilian, had shouted after me his last words, the end of his story when we were out of time and the train in motion. Only this: words. And here were two voices talking about the 'incident'.

'But what did that man want?'

'Seemed he was protesting about something . . .'

'He had it in for someone.'

'I would say he had it in for everyone.'

'I would say so, too; he was a deadbeat.'

'If I'd been down there I would have arrested him.'

They were two cigar-voices, loud, drawling, sweetened with dialect. They were speaking in Sicilian, in dialect.

I leaned my head out into the corridor and saw them at the window, two stout, solidly built men, in hats and overcoats, one with whiskers, the other without, two Sicilians who looked like lorry-drivers, but well-dressed, prosperous, pretentious in the way they held their necks and backs, yet with something feigned and clumsy about them which perhaps, deep down, came from timidity.

'Two baritones,' I said to myself. And one of them, in fact, the one without whiskers, did have a voice rather like that of a baritone, sinuous and singsong.

'You would only have done your duty,' he said.

The other, behind his whiskers, had a voice hoarse from cigars, but sweet with dialect.

'Naturally,' he said. 'I would only have done my duty.'

I pulled my head back into the compartment but kept on listening, thinking along with the variation of the voices, baritone and hoarse, of their two faces, one with whiskers, one without.

'That kind of man should always be arrested,' said Without Whiskers.

F 102, 158

'Really,' Whiskers said, 'you never know.'

'Every deadbeat is a dangerous man,' said Without Whiskers.

'Of course, he's capable of anything,' said Whiskers.

'Of stealing,' said Without Whiskers.

'That goes without saying,' said Whiskers.

'Of pulling big knives,' said Without Whiskers.

'Undoubtedly,' said Whiskers.

'Even of political crime,' said Without Whiskers.

They looked each other in the eye and smiled at each other, I could tell from the face of one and from the back of the other, and so they continued to talk, Whiskers and Without Whiskers, about what they meant by political crime. It seemed they meant lack of respect, of consideration, or so they said, and without resentment they accused all humanity, they said humanity was born to crime.

'In whatever class, in whatever part of society . . .' Whiskers said.

And Without Whiskers: 'Whether they're ignorant, whether they're educated . . .'

And Whiskers: 'Whether they're rich, whether they're poor . . .'

Without Whiskers: 'It makes no difference.'

Whiskers: 'Shopkeepers . . .'

Without Whiskers: 'Lawyers . . .'

Whiskers: 'My pork butcher, in Lodi . . .'

Without Whiskers: 'And in Bologna, a lawyer . . .'

Once again they looked each other in the eye, once

again they smiled at each other, once again I saw this from the face of one and the back of the other, and, despite the rattle of the train along the tracks between orange trees and the sea, I heard them tell each other about this pork butcher in Lodi and this lawyer in Bologna.

'You see,' said Whiskers, 'they don't have any respect.'

'They don't have any consideration,' said Without Whiskers.

And Whiskers: 'At Lodi, my barber . . .'

And Without Whiskers: 'My landlord, in Bologna . . .'

And they told one another about this barber in Lodi, this landlord in Bologna, and Whiskers said that once he had arrested his barber and kept him locked up for three days, and Without Whiskers said that he had done the same with his butcher in Bologna, and I could hear from their voices that they were satisfied, moved with satisfaction and almost at the point of throwing themselves on each other's necks in their common satisfaction with what they knew they were able to do: to arrest people and keep them locked up.

And they told one another other little facts, always without resentment, always mournfully, and having exhausted their satisfaction they became perplexed and asked each other why, after all, people gave them dirty looks.

'Because we're Sicilian,' said Whiskers.

'That's exactly what it is, because we're Sicilian,' said Without Whiskers.

They discussed being Sicilian in Lodi and being Sicilian in Bologna, and suddenly Without Whiskers let out a kind of cry of sorrow and said that at home, in Sicily, it was even worse.

'Oh yes, it's even worse,' said Whiskers.

And Without Whiskers: 'In Sciacca, I . . .'

And Whiskers: 'In Mussumeli, I . . .'

They said that it was worse in Sciacca and in Mussumeli, and Without Whiskers said his mother didn't tell people what he did for a living, she was ashamed to say it, and said instead that he worked in the Land Registry.

'The Land Registry!' he said.

'It's a matter of preconceptions,' said Whiskers.

'I know . . . old prejudices,' said Without Whiskers.

And they said that it was impossible to live in the countryside.

The train made a racket as it ran between the orange groves and the sea and Without Whiskers said: 'What beautiful orange trees!' And Whiskers said: 'What a beautiful sea!' And both said how beautiful it was in their towns, in Sciacca, in Mussumeli; but again they said one couldn't live there.

'I don't know why I go back,' said Whiskers.

'And do you think I do?' said Without Whiskers. 'I have a Bolognese wife, Bolognese children . . . And still . . .'

Whiskers said: 'As soon as I get permission, every year, without fail . . .'

Without Whiskers: 'Without fail . . . especially around Christmas.'

Whiskers: 'Especially in December. And for what?'

Without Whiskers: 'To rot one's guts.'

Whiskers: 'To poison one's blood.'

Here the door of the compartment was closed with force, I'd say slammed, by someone who sat across from me.

The voices disappeared, cut off all at once, by the noise of the tracks. And the train flew through the groves of orange trees, into tunnels, alongside the sea. A snowy high peak, far away, appeared and disappeared; the sky was clear, washed clean by the wind, without more rain though still sunless; and I recognised this route, I could tell that we were halfway between Messina and Catania. And I could no longer hear the two voices outside; I looked around, eager for other Sicilians.

VI

'Didn't you smell the stink?' said the man sitting across from me.

He was a Sicilian, a big man, a Lombard or Norman perhaps from Nicosia, and he too looked like a lorry-driver like the owners of the voices in the corridor, but genuine, open, and tall, with blue eyes. Not young but about fifty, and I thought that my father would maybe now resemble him, even though I remembered my father young, spry and thin, dressed in red and black, reciting *Macbeth*. This man must have been from Nicosia or Aidone; he spoke a dialect which to this day is quasi-Lombard, with a Lombard 'u', from those Lombard places of Val Demone: Nicosia or Aidone.

'Didn't you smell the stink?' he asked.

He had a little salt and pepper beard, blue eyes, an olympian forehead. He was without a jacket in the cold third-class compartment and maybe he looked like a lorry-driver only because of that and not for any other reason. He wrinkled his nose above the sparse hair of his moustache and beard, for he was hairy like an old man; without a jacket, in shirt-sleeves, with little dark checks on his shirt, and a huge brown jacket with six pockets.

'Stink? What stink?' I asked.

'What? You didn't smell it?' he said.

'I don't know,' I responded. 'I don't know what stink you're talking about.'

'Oh!' he said. 'He doesn't know what stink I'm talking about.'

And he turned towards the others in the compartment.

There were three others.

One, a young man with a beret of thin cloth, wrapped up in a shawl, was yellow-faced, wasted, very small; he sat at an angle to me, against the window.

Another, also young, was red-faced, strong, with crinkly black hair and a black neck, a low-class man

from the city, definitely from Catania, and he sat at the
other end of my bench, across from the sick boy.

Between the big Lombard and the sick boy was a
little old man without a hair on his face, and dark,
and incredibly small and thin: a dry leaf. His skin was
tough and square-scaled like a turtle's. He had got on at
Roccalumera and was sitting, if one could call it sitting,
on the edge of the bench with the wooden armrests
pressing against his back. He could have raised them
but hadn't.

To him in particular the big Lombard spoke, when he
turned towards the others.

'He doesn't know what stink I'm talking about!' said
the Big Lombard.

A sound came like a puff, the beginning of a whistle,
but deadened, without the body of a voice: 'Heh!' And
it was the little old man who laughed. But it was not only
now that he was laughing. He had been laughing with his
eyes from the moment he got on board; with eyes which
were penetrating, alive, laughing steadily as they looked
around him, at me, at the bench, at the young man from
Catania, laughing continually: he was happy.

'Incredible! He doesn't know what stink I'm talking
about,' said the Big Lombard.

Everyone looked at me, and they found it hilarious,
even the sick boy with the dreary silent hilarity of
the sick.

'Oh!' I said, finding it hilarious, too. 'I really don't
understand. I don't smell any stink.'

Then the man from Catania broke in.

He bent forward, red-faced, with his big curly head, thick in his thighs and arms, wearing enormous shoes, and he said:

'He's talking about the stink that was coming from the corridor.'

'There was a stink from the corridor?' I asked.

'Come on, it's incredible,' shouted the Big Lombard. 'You didn't smell it?'

And the man from Catania said: 'He's talking about the stink of those two . . .'

'Those two?' I asked. 'Those two at the window? They made a stink? What stink?'

Again I heard the dead sound, without the body of a voice, of the tiny old man and I saw that his mouth was open like the slit in a piggybank. I also saw the sick boy, impassive in his silent hilarity, wrapped in his shawl; and I saw the Big Lombard practically furious, but also jolly in those eyes which seemed to be the blue eyes of my father.

I understood then what the stink was and laughed.

'Oh, the stink!' I said. 'The stink!'

Everyone was cheerful and satisfied, reconciled, while in the corridor those two were returning to the places where they'd been children, to their hometowns.

'It's strange,' I said. 'There's no place on earth where they're more hated than in Sicily. Yet in Italy it's almost all Sicilians who do that job.'

'All Sicilians?' the Big Lombard exclaimed.

'Really!' I said. 'For the past fifteen years I've moved around Italy. I've lived in Florence, I've lived in Bologna, in Turin, and now I live in Milan, and everywhere I've met another Sicilian that was his job.'

'Right, that's what my cousin who travels says,' observed the man from Catania.

And the Big Lombard said:

'Well, it's understandable. We're a sad people, we are.'

'Sad?' I said, and I looked at the little old man with the hilarious little face, his little eyes swimming with hilarity.

'Very sad,' said the Big Lombard. 'Even lugubrious. We're always ready, all of us, to see the blackest side of things . . .'

I looked at the little face of the old man, and didn't say anything, and the Big Lombard continued: 'Always hoping for something else, something better, and always despairing of being able to have it . . . Always distressed. Always beaten. And deep down, always tempted to take our own lives.'

'Yes, that's true,' said the man from Catania earnestly.

And he began to consider the tips of his enormous shoes. And I, without taking my eyes off the little face of the old man, said: 'That could be true. But what does that have to do with doing that job?'

And the Big Lombard said: 'I think it has something to do with it, for some reason. I think it has something to do with it. I don't know how to explain it, but I think it has something to do with it. What do you do when you give up? When you decide you're doomed? You do the thing you hate most. I think that must be it. I think it's understandable that they're almost all Sicilians.'

VII

Then the Big Lombard recounted his own story. He was coming from Messina, where he had visited a specialist for a particular kidney ailment, and was returning home to Leonforte, he was from Leonforte, in the Val Demone between Enna and Nicosia. He was a landlord with three beautiful daughters so he said, three beautiful daughters, and he had a horse on which he rode over his land, and at one time he believed – since this was a tall, proud horse – at one time he believed himself to be a king; but that didn't seem to him to be the whole story, believing himself a king while mounted on a horse, and he wanted to acquire another understanding, so he said, acquire another understanding, and to feel different about himself, to feel something new in his soul; he would give everything he possessed, even his horse and his land, just to feel more at peace with other men – like someone, so he said, like someone who has nothing to repent.

'Not that I have anything in particular to repent,' he said. 'Not at all. And I don't even mean it in the religious sense. But I don't feel at peace with other men.'

He wanted to have a fresh conscience, so he said, a fresh conscience which would require him to carry out other duties, not the usual ones, but new duties and higher ones towards men, because there was no satisfaction in carrying out the usual ones and one ended up feeling as if one had done nothing, dissatisfied, disappointed in oneself.

'I think a man matures by doing something else,' he said. 'Not only by not stealing, not killing, and so forth, by being a good citizen . . . I think one matures by doing something else, by taking on new, different duties. That's what we all feel, I think, the absence of other duties, other tasks to carry out . . . Tasks which would satisfy our conscience, in a new sense.'

He fell silent, and the man from Catania spoke: 'Yes, sir,' he said.

And looked at the huge tips of his shoes.

'Yes,' he said. 'I think you're right.'

And red-faced, full of health, he looked at his shoes, yet with the sadness of a vigorous but unsatisfied animal, a horse or an ox; and once again he said 'Yes', convinced, persuaded, as if he had been given a name for his illness, and he didn't say anything more, didn't say anything about himself, only added:

'Are you a professor?'

'Me, a professor?' the Big Lombard exclaimed.

And the little old man next to him made his sound of a dry leaf, without the body of a voice, his 'Heh!' He seemed to be a piece of dry straw trying to speak.

'Heh!' he went. 'Heh!'

Twice. And he had penetrating eyes swimming with laughter in his little face which was scaly and dark like the dry shell of a turtle.

'Heh!' he went with his mouth like the slit of a piggy-bank.

'It's nothing to laugh about, Dad, nothing to laugh about,' the Big Lombard said, turning towards him, and again he told the story, from the beginning, of his trip to Messina, his holdings above Leonforte, his three daughters each one more beautiful than the others, and of his tall proud horse, and of his not feeling at peace with other men and how he believed he wanted a new conscience, and new duties to carry out, in order to feel more at peace with other men – all, this time, exclusively for the benefit of the little old man who looked at him and laughed and went 'Heh!' the sound of the beginning of a whistle, without the body of a voice.

'But why,' said the Big Lombard at a certain point, 'why are you sitting so uncomfortably? You can raise this.'

And he raised the wooden armrest against which the little old man was sitting on the edge of his seat.

'See, you can raise this,' the Big Lombard said.

And the little old man turned around and looked at the raised wooden armrest and again went 'Heh!' a couple of times, his scaly little hands holding on to a knotty walking stick almost as tall as himself, with a knob shaped like a serpent's head.

It was when he moved to turn around to look at the armrest that I saw the serpent's head, and then I saw something green in the mouth of this serpent's head, the three little leaves of an orange twig, and the little old man saw me and again went 'Heh!' and took the orange twig and put it in his own mouth, in his mouth like the slit of a piggybank, so that he, too, was a serpent's head.

'Ah, I think that's exactly it,' said the Big Lombard, speaking now to everyone in general. 'We don't find satisfaction any longer in doing our duty, our duties . . . It makes no difference to us. We feel bad all the same. And I think that's exactly it . . . Because they are old duties, too old, they've become too easy, they no longer mean anything to the conscience . . .'

'You're not a professor, really?' said the man from Catania.

He was red-faced, an ox, and with an ox's sadness he was still looking at his shoes.

'Me, a professor?' said the Big Lombard. 'I seem like a professor? I'm not ignorant, I can read a book, if I want to, but I'm not a professor. I was educated by the Salesians as a boy, but I'm not a professor.'

Thus we arrived at the last station before Catania, already in the suburbs of the great city of black stone, and the old man who went 'Heh!' like a dry piece of straw got off; and then we arrived in Catania. There was sun on the streets of black stone that we passed, streets and houses, black stone jutting out beneath the train, and we arrived at Catania station, and the man from Catania got off and the Big Lombard also got off and, facing the window, I could see that Whiskers and Without Whiskers had also got off.

Everyone on the train got off, and the journey continued with the few remaining carriages empty in the sun, and I asked myself why I hadn't got off too.

Anyway, I had a ticket for Siracusa, and so I continued the journey in the empty carriage, in the sun, across an empty plain. And returning from the corridor I was surprised to find, still in his place, wrapped in his shawl, with his thin cloth beret on his head, the young man with the waxy yellow complexion of illness; and with him, looking at him looking at me without a word, but happy to be with him, I journeyed on and on, in the sun across the empty plain, until the plain was covered with malarial green, and we reached Lentini, at the foot of the long green slopes of oranges and malaria, and the young man wrapped in the shawl got off and, wasted by malaria, stiffened with cold in the sun on the deserted pavement.

So I was alone for the journey through the rocky countryside towards Siracusa on the coast. But then I raised my eyes and outside in the corridor, standing still, Without Whiskers was watching me.

VIII

He smiled.

He stood in the corridor with his shoulders in the sun, with the countryside of rocks and sea behind his shoulders, and it was just the two of us in the whole carriage, perhaps in the whole train, en route through the empty countryside.

He smiled at me with his cigar-smoking face, moustache-less and fat in his aubergine-coloured overcoat, his aubergine-coloured hat, and he came in and sat down.

'May I?' he asked, when he was already seated.

'Go right ahead,' I responded. 'Of course.'

And he was happy to be able to sit there with my permission, happy not just to sit down, there was a whole train car to sit in; but to sit there, where I was, another person, another human being.

'I thought I saw you get off at Catania,' I observed.

'Oh, you saw me?' he said, happily. 'I was accompanying a friend of mine to the train for Caltanissetta. I got back on at the last minute.'

'I see,' I said.

'I got back on the last carriage.'

'I see,' I said.

'I barely made it in time.'

'I see,' I said.

'There were first-class and second-class carriages in

the middle,' he said. 'And I had to stay there, far from my bags.'

And I said, 'I see.'

'But at Lentini I got off and came here,' he said.

And once again I said: 'I see.'

And he didn't say anything more, he was quiet for a moment, happy, satisfied to have explained everything. Then he sighed, smiled and said:

'I was worried about my bags!'

'Of course,' I said. 'One never knows.'

'That's true, eh?' he said. 'One never knows . . . What with these nasty characters around . . .'

'Of course,' I said. 'With these nasty characters . . .'

'Like the one who got off at Lentini,' he said. 'Did you see him?'

'Who?' I said. 'The one all wrapped up?'

'Yes,' he said. 'The one all wrapped up. Didn't he have the face of a criminal?'

I didn't respond, and he sighed, and looked around, and read all the little enamelled signs in the compartment, and looked at the empty countryside, curving, speeding past us, just more of the same barren rock along the sea, and then finally he smiled and said:

'I work in the Land Registry.'

'Oh!' I said. 'Really? And what are you doing? Going home on holiday?'

'Yes,' he said. 'I'm on leave . . . I'm going to Sciacca, in the country.'

'To Sciacca,' I said. 'And have you come from far away?'

'From Bologna,' he said. 'That's where I work. And my wife is Bolognese. My children, too.'

He was happy. And I said:

'And you're going to Sciacca from here?'

'Yes, from here,' he said. 'Siracusa, Spaccaforno, Modica, Genisi, Donnafugata . . .'

'Vittoria, Falconara,' I said. 'Licata.'

'Ah ha!' he said. 'Girgenti . . .'

'Agrigento, actually,' I said. 'But wouldn't it have been easier for you to go through Caltanissetta?'

'Sure, it would have been easier,' he said. 'And I'd have saved eight lire. But from here it's all along the sea . . .'

'You like the sea?' I asked him.

'I don't know,' he said. 'I think I do like it. Anyway, I like going this way . . .'

And he sighed, and smiled, then stood and said:

'Excuse me.'

He went into the next compartment and came back with a little lunchbox like those for snacks for children, but made of cardboard, and he put it on his knees, on his short legs, opened it, took out some bread and smiled.

'Bread,' he said. 'Heh! Heh!'

Then he took out a long omelette and smiled once again. 'Omelette!' he said.

I smiled at him in response. And he cut the omelette in two pieces with a pen-knife, and offered me a piece.

'No, thanks,' I said, shielding myself from his hand armed with omelette.

His face darkened.

'What?' he said. 'You don't want any?'

'I'm not hungry!' I said.

And he: 'You're not hungry? Travelling always makes one hungry.'

And I: 'But it's not even one o'clock yet. I'll eat in Siracusa.'

And he: 'Fine. You can start now. In Siracusa you can eat some more.'

And I: 'But I can't. It would spoil my appetite.'

And his face darkened even more. He insisted.

'I work in the Land Registry!' he said again. And he said: 'Don't insult me this way! Please accept.'

I accepted and ate the omelette with him, and he was delighted. Somehow, I was delighted too; happy to make him happy by chewing and getting my hands dirty with omelette just like him. And meanwhile we passed Augusta, its abandoned houses on the mountain in the middle of the sea among the aeroplanes and ships, between the salt marshes, under the sun; and we were nearing Siracusa, journeying through the empty countryside along the bay of Siracusa.

'You'll have more of an appetite in Siracusa,' he said. And he added: 'Are you getting off there?'

'I get off there,' I replied.

'Do you live there?' he said.

'No,' I replied. 'I don't live there.'

'You don't know anyone in Siracusa?' he said.

'No,' I replied.

'You're going there on business, then,' he said.

'No,' I replied. 'I'm not.'

He looked at me, baffled, as he ate his omelette and as he looked at me eating his omelette, I said:

'You have a fine baritone voice.'

Immediately he blushed.

'Oh!' he said.

'What? You didn't know?' I said.

'Oh, I know, sure,' he said, red and happy.

And I said, 'Naturally. You couldn't have lived this long without knowing. Too bad you work in the Land Registry instead of singing . . .'

'You're right,' he said. 'I would have loved it . . . in *Falstaff*, in *Rigoletto* . . . on all the stages of Europe.'

'Or even in the street, what difference does it make? It's still better than being an ordinary man,' I said.

'Oh, sure, maybe . . .' he said.

And he was silent, a little disconcerted, and he kept chewing in silence, and behind the curve of the rocky countryside the rock of the Dome of Siracusa appeared, against the sea.

'Here we are in Siracusa,' I said.

He looked at me and smiled.

'So you've arrived,' he observed.

We said goodbye as the train entered the station.

'I think I'll just make my connection in time,' he said.

And I got off in Siracusa, the place where I was born and from which I'd departed fifteen years before, one of the stations of my life. Unloading his bags, the man who said he worked in the Land Registry – that is, Without Whiskers – greeted me once again.

'So long,' he said. 'What'll you be doing in Siracusa?'

I was already far enough away not to respond and I didn't, but headed towards the exit and didn't see him again.

I was in Siracusa.

But what would I do in Siracusa? Why had I come to Siracusa? Why had I bought a ticket to Siracusa instead of to somewhere else? It certainly didn't make any difference to me where I was going. And certainly whether I was in Siracusa, or somewhere else, didn't make any difference. It was all the same to me. I was in Sicily. I was visiting Sicily. And I could just as well get back on the train and go back home.

But I had come to know the man with the oranges, With Whiskers and Without Whiskers, the Big Lombard, the man from Catania, the little old man with the voice of a dry piece of straw, the young malaria victim wrapped in his shawl, and it seemed to me that maybe it did make some difference whether I was in Siracusa or somewhere else.

'What an idiot,' I said to myself. 'Why didn't I go to see my mother instead? For the same amount of money, in the same amount of time, I could have been in the mountains . . .'

And I found myself with the unsent greeting card for my mother in my hand, and I realised it was already the

eighth of December. 'Damn!' I thought. 'Poor old lady!
If I don't take it to her myself it won't get to her in time.'
And I went to the station of the branch railway to see if
I still had enough money to continue my journey as far
as my mother's house, in the mountains.

Part Two

IX

At three o'clock in the December sun, leaving the sea, now hidden, crackling behind it, the miniature train of little green wagons entered a tunnel in the rock and then a forest of prickly pears. This was Sicily's branch railway between Siracusa and the mountains: Sortino, Palazzolo, Monte Lauro, Vizzini, Grammichele.

We began to pass the stations, wooden huts where the sun was shining on the red hats of the stationmasters, and the forest opened and closed up again with tall prickly pear cacti like pitchforks. They were as if carved from skyblue stone, all these prickly pears, and when we passed a living soul it was a boy who was going or coming, along the tracks, to pick the fruit crowned with thorns that grew, like coral, on the stone of the prickly pear branches. He shouted when the train went by him.

A wind blew through the quarries of the forest; one could hear it when the train stopped, a tiny crackling wind just as I'd heard earlier near the sea. Then a strip of red flag fluttered, we arrived, we left again. And between the prickly pears, houses appeared; the train stopped on the arches of a bridge and from the bridge passed over a slope of roofs; we went through a tunnel, and once again we were between prickly pears and rock cliffs, and once again we didn't pass another living soul except for a boy.

He shouted, shouted at the train, when the train went by him; and there was sun on his shouting, on the strips of red flags, on the red hats of the stationmasters.

Then suddenly a red hat, a red flag, a boy's shout were no longer in sunlight, and under the prickly pears it was dark, a light was lit. A grey donkey forded a run-off of water, and the train ascended and passed through tunnels. One could see the long spine of mountains and when the train stopped, down in a valley, one could see four lights, five lights – the towns.

Then one could hear the roar of a stream and a voice said, 'We're in Vizzini.' And the roar of the stream remained fixed at the foot of the train, we had stopped. Then we got off alongside the water, it was fully night, and on one side there was the mountain, on the other the sky.

That was Vizzini and there I passed the night in a room at the inn, which smelled of carob trees. There were no more buses to my destination that night, and it didn't make any difference to me not to have caught the bus, the only thing that mattered was to sleep, and so I slept there, slept under that smell of carob as deeply as the dead. And I got up the next day full of carob, too, with that smell now in me, in the light which came through the shutterless windows. And I journeyed, as if still sleeping, by bus along the stream, from Vizzini high up over three deep ravines, heading higher into the mountains for three hours, until someone said, 'Snow,' and we had arrived.

X

'How about that, I'm at my mother's,' I thought when I got off the bus, at the foot of the long flight of steps that led to the highest reaches of my mother's town.

The name of the town was inscribed on a wall just as it appeared on the cards I sent every year to my mother, and everything else, this flight of steps between old houses, the mountains all around, the clumps of snow on the roofs, was there before my eyes just as I suddenly remembered having seen it, once or twice, during my childhood. And it seemed to make some difference to me to be there, and I was glad to have come, not to have stayed in Siracusa, not to have taken the train back again to Northern Italy, not to have finished my journey yet. That was the most important thing: not to have finished my journey yet, maybe even to have just started out. This way, at least, I felt something, as I looked at the long flight of steps and the houses and the church domes high up, the overhangs of houses and rock, and the roofs in the ravine below, the smoke from a chimney, the clumps of snow, the straw, and the little crowd of Sicilian children barefoot on the crust of ice on the ground, around the cast-iron fountain in the sun.

'How about that, I'm at my mother's,' I thought again, and it was as if I had arrived there spontaneously, just as spontaneously as one finds oneself in a certain place in memory – or even more fantastical, as if I had begun travelling in the fourth dimension. It seemed there was nothing, only a dream, a spiritual intermission, between being in Siracusa and being there in my mother's town; it seemed I had arrived there just by resolving to go, through a motion of memory, not of my body; and thus the morning of being there, the cold of the mountain, and the pleasure of it; and I didn't even regret not being there the night before, in time for my mother's name-day, as if this light were not that of December 9th but still that of December 8th, or of a day in a fourth dimension.

I knew my mother lived in the highest part of town, I remembered climbing these steps as a child, when I came to visit my grandparents, and I began to climb. There were faggots of wood on the steps in front of some of the houses, and I continued up, and every once in a while there was a hem of snow round the steps, and in the cold, in the morning sun (by now it was almost noon), I finally arrived at the top, overlooking the vast mountain town and the ravines mottled with snow. There was no one around, only barefoot children, their feet ulcered with chilblains, and I made my way between the houses high up round the dome of the big

Mother Church, which I also recognised, as ancient as I remembered it.

I made my way holding the greeting card on which was written the name of the street and the number of the house where my mother lived, and I was able to find my way very easily, guided by the greeting card like a postman, and guided a bit by memory, too. I also asked, because I wanted to, at some little grocery stores I saw, filled with sacks and barrels. And so I came to visit Mrs Concezione Ferrauto, my mother, looking for her as if I were a postman, with the greeting card in my hand and her name, Concezione Ferrauto, on my lips. The house was the last one on its street, astride a little garden, with a short flight of steps outside. I went up them in the sun, looking once more at the address on the card, and I was at my mother's, I knew the doorway and it did make some difference to me to be there, it was all the more fully a journey in the fourth dimension.

I pushed open the door and entered the house and from another room a voice said, 'Who is it?' And I recognised that voice, after fifteen years of not remembering it; it was the same voice I now recalled from fifteen years before, high and clear, and I remembered the childhood sound of my mother talking from another room.

'Signora Concezione,' I said.

XI

The lady of the house appeared, tall and white-haired, and I recognised my mother perfectly, a tall woman with nearly blonde chestnut-brown hair, and a sharp chin, sharp nose, dark eyes. She had a red shawl over her shoulders to keep herself warm.

I laughed. 'Happy name-day,' I said.

'Oh, it's Silvestro,' my mother said, and came close.

I gave her a kiss on the cheek. She kissed me on the cheek and said, 'But what the devil brings you here?'

'How did you recognise me?' I said.

My mother laughed. 'I'm asking myself the same thing,' she said. The room smelled of roasting herring, and my mother added, 'Let's go into the kitchen . . . I have herring on the fire!'

We went into the next room where the sun struck the dark iron bedstead, and from there into the little kitchen where the sun struck everything. On the ground, beneath a wooden platform, a copper brazier was lit. The herring was roasting over it, smoking, and my mother bent over to turn it. 'You'll taste how good it is,' she said.

'I will,' I said, and breathed in the smell of herring, and it made a difference to me, I liked it, it brought back the smell of the meals of my childhood. 'I can't imagine anything better,' I said, and asked, 'Did we have it when I was a boy?'

'Oh yes,' my mother said. 'Herring in the winter and peppers in the summer. That's what we always had. Don't you remember?'

'And fava beans with thistles,' I said, remembering.

'Yes,' my mother said. 'Fava beans with thistles. You loved fava beans with thistles.'

'Oh,' I said. 'I loved them?'

And my mother: 'You'd always want a second helping . . . And the same thing with lentils done with artichoke, sundried tomatoes, and lard . . .'

'And a sprig of rosemary, yes?' I said.

And my mother: 'Yes . . . And a sprig of rosemary.'

And I: 'I always wanted a second helping of that, too?'

And my mother: 'Oh yes! You were like Esau . . . You would have given away your birthright for a second plate of lentils . . . I can still see you when you came home from school, at three or four in the afternoon, on the train . . .'

'That's right,' I said, 'on the freight train, in the baggage compartment . . . First me by myself, then me and Felice, then me, Felice and Liborio . . .'

'All of you so sweet,' my mother said. 'With your heads thick with hair, your little faces black, your hands always black . . . And right away you'd ask: are there lentils today, mamma?'

'We were living in those plate-layers' houses then,' I said. 'We'd get off the train at the station, at San Cataledo, at Serradifalco, at Acquaviva, all those places we lived, and we had to walk a mile or two to get home.'

And my mother: 'Yes, sometimes three. When the train passed, I knew you were on the way, along the tracks, and I'd heat up the lentils, roast the herring, and then I'd hear you shout, "Land! Land!"'

'"Land"? Why "land"?' I asked.

'Yes, "land"! It was some game you played,' my mother said. 'And then once, in Racalmuto, the plate-layer's house was up an incline and the train had to slow down, and you'd worked out how to jump off the train while it was moving so you could get off in front of the house. And I had a black fear you'd end up under the wheels, so I'd wait outside for you with a cane . . .'

'And you'd spank us?'

And my mother: 'Oh yes! Don't you remember? I could've broken your legs with that cane. I even made you go without dinner, sometimes.'

She got up again, holding the herring by the tail to examine it on one side, then the other; and as I smelled the herring I saw that her face had lost nothing of the young face it had once been, as I was remembering it now, but age had added something to it. This was my mother: the memory of her fifteen years earlier, twenty years earlier, young and terrifying, the cane in her hand as she waited for us to jump off the freight train; that memory, plus all the time that had passed since then, the something-more of the present. In short, she was twice real. She examined the herring on one side then the other, holding it up, and even the herring was both a memory and the something-more of the present – the sun, the cold, the copper brazier in the middle of the kitchen, the existence in my mind of that place in the world where I found myself, everything had this quality of being twice real; and maybe this was why it made a difference to me to be there, to be on a journey, because of everything that was twice real, even the journey down from Messina, and the oranges on the ferry, and the Big Lombard on the train, and Whiskers and Without Whiskers, and the malarial green, and Siracusa – in all, Sicily itself, everything twice real, and on a journey in the fourth dimension.

XII

The herring was filleted, put on a plate, sprinkled with oil, and my mother and I sat at the table. In the kitchen, that is; with the sun shining through the window behind my mother's shoulders wrapped in the red shawl and her very light chestnut-brown hair. The table was against the wall, and my mother and I sat across from each other, with the brazier beneath the table, and on top of it the plate of herring almost overflowing with olive oil. And my mother tossed me a napkin, reached over with a plate and a fork, and pulled from the breadbox a large half-eaten loaf of bread.

'Do you mind if I don't put out a tablecloth?' she asked.

'Of course not,' I said.

And she: 'I can't do the wash every day ... I'm old now.'

But when I was a child we always ate without a tablecloth, except for Sundays and holidays, and I remembered my mother always saying she couldn't wash every day. I began to eat the herring with bread, and asked: 'There's no soup?'

My mother looked at me and said, 'Who knew you were coming?'

And I looked at her, and said: 'But I mean for you. You don't make soup for yourself?'

'You mean for me?' my mother said. 'I've hardly ever eaten soup in my life. I made it for you and your father, but for me, this is what I always ate: herring in the winter, roasted peppers in the summer, lots of oil, lots of bread ...'

'Always?'

'Always. Why not?' my mother said. 'Olives, too, of course, and sometimes pork chops, or sausage, when we had a pig ...'

'We had a pig?' I asked.

'Don't you remember?' my mother said. 'Some years we kept a pig and raised it on prickly pears, then we butchered it ...'

Then I remembered the countryside around a plate-layer's house with the railway track, and the prickly pears, and the snorts of a pig. We were well-off in those plate-layers' houses, I thought. We had all the countryside to run around in, without having to farm it, without farmers around, only an occasional sheep and the sulphur miners who came by on their way back from the sulphur mines at night, when we were already in bed. We were well-off, I thought, and asked: 'Didn't we also have chickens?'

My mother said yes, of course, we did have a few, and I said: 'We made mustard . . .'

And my mother: 'We made all kinds of things . . . sun-dried tomatoes . . . prickly pear biscuits.'

'We were well-off,' I said, and I believed it, thinking of the tomatoes drying in the sun on summer afternoons without a living soul in the whole countryside. It was dry country, the colour of sulphur, and I remembered the great buzzing of summer and the welling up of silence, and I thought once again that we were well-off. 'We were well-off,' I said. 'We had wire screens.'

'They were malarial places, for the most part,' my mother said.

'That mighty malaria!' I said.

And my mother: 'Mighty is right!'

And I: 'With the cicadas!' And I thought of the forest of cicadas there on the metal screens in the windows that looked out onto the veranda, in that loneliness of sunlight, and I said: 'I thought malaria meant the cicadas!'

My mother laughed. 'Maybe that's why you caught so many of them?'

'I caught them?' I asked. 'But it was their singing I thought was malaria, not them . . . I'd catch them?'

'Oh yes!' my mother said. 'Twenty, thirty at a time.'

And I: 'I must've caught them thinking they were crickets.' And I asked: 'What did I do with them?'

My mother laughed again. 'I think you ate them,' she said.

'I ate them?' I exclaimed.

'Yes,' my mother said. 'You and your brothers.'

She laughed and I was disconcerted. 'How could that be?'

And my mother said: 'Maybe you were hungry.'

And I: 'We were hungry?'

And my mother: 'Maybe so.'

'But we were well-off, in our house!' I protested.

My mother looked at me. 'Yes,' she said. 'Your father got paid at the end of every month, and so for ten days we were well-off, we were the envy of all the farmers and sulphur miners . . . But when the first ten days were up, we were in the same boat as them. We ate snails.'

'Snails?' I said.

'Yes, and wild chicory,' my mother said.

And I said: 'The others ate only snails?'

And my mother: 'Yes, poor people ate only snails, most of the time. And we were poor the last twenty days of every month.'

And I: 'We ate snails for twenty days?'

And my mother: 'Snails and wild chicory.'

I thought about it, smiled, and said: 'But I bet they were pretty good, anyway.'

And my mother: 'Delicious. You can cook them so many ways.'

And I: 'What do you mean, so many ways?'

And my mother: 'Just boiled, for example. Or with garlic and tomato. Or breaded and fried.'

And I: 'What a thought! Breaded and fried? In the shell?'

And my mother: 'Of course! You eat them by sucking them out of the shell . . . Don't you remember?'

And I: 'I remember, I remember . . . Seems to me sucking the shell is the best part.'

And my mother: 'Hours can go by, just sucking . . .'

XIII

For two or three minutes we sat in silence, eating the herring, then my mother began to talk again, telling me a few ways to cook snails. So I could teach my wife, she said. But my wife didn't cook snails, I told her. And my mother wanted to know what my wife usually cooked, and I told her she usually made something boiled.

'Boiled? Boiled what?' my mother exclaimed.

'Boiled meat,' I said.

'Meat? What kind of meat?' my mother exclaimed.

'Beef,' I said.

My mother looked at me with disgust. She asked me how it tasted. And I told her that it didn't have any particular taste, that we ate pasta in the broth.

'And the meat?' my mother asked me.

And I told her, truthfully, that there usually wasn't any meat after we ate the broth. I explained it all: the carrots, the celery, the piece of bone we called meat; explaining everything accurately so she would understand that in Northern Italy we were much better off than in Sicily, at least nowadays, in the city at least, and that we ate more or less like Christians.

My mother was still looking at me with disgust.

'Oh!' she exclaimed. 'Every day, that's what you eat?'

And I said: 'Yes! Not just Sundays! When one is working and earning money, at least!'

My mother was disconcerted. 'Every day! And don't you get bored?' she said.

'Don't you get bored with herring?' I said.

'But herring is tasty,' my mother said. And she began to tell me how much herring she thought she had eaten in her life, and how, in her capacity for eating herring and more herring, she was like her father, my grandfather.

'I think herring has something good for the brain,' she said. 'It gives you a good complexion, too.' And she pointed out all the good she thought herring did for various human organs and functions; maybe it was really thanks to herring, she declared, that my grandfather was a great man.

'He was a great man, Grandpa?' I asked. I vaguely remembered having grown up, in my most distant childhood, under a shadow; it must have been the shadow of the greatness of my grandfather. I asked: 'He was a great man, Grandpa?'

'Oh yes! You didn't know that?' my mother said.

I said yes, I knew, but I wanted to know what he had done that was great, and my mother shouted that he was great in every way. He had brought into the world daughters who were tall and beautiful, all daughters, she shouted, and had built this house where she now lived, without even being a mason, with his own hands.

'He was a great man,' she said. 'He could work eighteen hours a day, and he was a great socialist, a great hunter and great on horseback in the procession on Saint Joseph's Day.'

'He rode in the procession on Saint Joseph's Day?' I said.

'Oh yes! He was a great horseman, better than anyone else in this town, or in Piazza Armerina,' my mother said. 'How could they have had a cavalcade without him?'

And I said: 'But he was a socialist?'

And my mother: 'He was a socialist . . . He didn't know how to read or write, but he understood politics and he was a socialist . . .'

And I: 'But how could he ride behind Saint Joseph if he was a socialist? Socialists don't believe in Saint Joseph.'

'What a beast you are!' my mother said then. 'Your grandfather wasn't just a socialist like all the others. He was a great man. He could believe in Saint Joseph and still be a socialist. He could hold a thousand things in his head at the same time. And he was a socialist because he understood politics . . . But he could believe in Saint Joseph. He never said anything against Saint Joseph.'

'But the priests, I imagine, must have thought there was a contradiction,' I said.

And my mother: 'And what did he care about priests?'

And I: 'But the procession was the business of priests!'

'You really are an idiot!' my mother exclaimed. 'It was a procession of horses and men on horses. It was a caval-cade.' She got up and went to the window, and I understood that I was meant to follow her there. 'You see,' she said. The window overlooked the slope of roofs and then the ravines, the stream, and the woods in the winter sun, and the mountain with its rockface mottled with snow. 'You see,' my mother said. And I looked more closely, at those roofs with smokeless chimneys, and the stream, the carob woods, the spots of snow; more closely, that is, seeing them twice real, and my mother said:

'The procession started from there, across from us, and went towards that telegraph pole . . . There's a little church you can't see from here, on that mountain, but they would light it up inside and outside and it would look like a star. The cavalcade left from the church, with lanterns and bells, and went down the mountain. It was always at night, of course. We could see the lights and I knew my father was there at the head, a great horseman, with everyone waiting in the piazza down below or on the bridge. And the cavalcade entered the woods, we couldn't see the lanterns any more, we could only hear the bells. It went on for a long time and then the cavalcade appeared on the bridge, with all the noise of the bells, and the lanterns, and him at the head as if he felt like a king . . .'

'I think I remember,' I said, and in fact it seemed I'd at least dreamed something similar, the ringing bells of horses and a great star in front of the mountain, in the heart of the night, but my mother said: 'Nonsense! You were just three the only time you saw it.'

And I looked again at that Sicily outside, then at my mother all wrapped up in her shawl, from her light-haired head to her feet, and I saw she was wearing men's shoes, my father's old plate-layer's shoes, ankle high and maybe with studs, like the ones I remembered she always had the habit of wearing in the house, so as to be more comfortable, or to feel herself in some sense rooted in a man, and a bit of a man herself, a rib of man.

XIV

We sat down at the table again and as I looked at her without speaking, she said:

'What are you looking at?'

And I said: 'Can't I look at you?'

'Yes,' my mother said. 'If you want to look, look, but finish eating . . .' I cut another slice of bread, which had a hard, white crust as if poorly cooked, and said, 'So what gave Papa the idea to go off with another woman, at his age?'

My mother seemed surprised, offended even, as if she wanted to object to something in each of my words. 'What do you know about it?' she cried.

'He wrote to me,' I said.

'Oh, the coward!' my mother cried. 'He wrote to you that he saw another woman, and jilted me, and went off with her?'

I said yes, that was what I had understood, and she cried: 'What a coward!'

And I said: 'Why? It's not true?'

And my mother: 'How could it be true? You don't remember what a coward he was?'

'Coward?' I said.

'Oh yes,' my mother cried. 'Whenever he hit me he would start to cry and beg forgiveness . . .'

I burst out: 'Oh! He probably didn't like doing it.'

'He didn't like it!' my mother cried. 'As if I didn't know how to defend myself, as if I didn't give it right back to him . . . Maybe that's what he didn't like.'

I laughed. I laughed, and remembered him, my father, as slender as a boy, with his blue eyes, and my mother, heavy, strong, with her big shoes, the two of them wrestling until they got like wild beasts and hit each other, hitting everything, kicking the chairs, punching the windowpanes, cudgelling the table, and we laughed and applauded. I laughed. And my mother said:

'You know what a coward he was? Even when I was giving birth he cried. I was the one in pain, but I didn't cry, he cried. I would have liked to see my father in his place!'

'I imagine he didn't like seeing you suffer,' I said.

'He didn't like it!' my mother cried. 'Why did it have to bother him? I wasn't dying. It would've been better if he'd lifted a finger to help me instead of crying . . .'

And I: 'What could he have done?'

And my mother: 'What do you mean, what could he have done? You don't do a thing, when your wife gives birth?'

And I: 'Well, I hold her . . .'

'See, you do do something!' my mother said. 'But he didn't even hold me . . . We were alone in those lonely places, and there was so much to do, hot water to prepare, but he only knew how to cry . . . Or run to that railway hut nearby to call the women from there . . . That he liked, having other women in the house. But they never came right away, and I needed help, I shouted at him to help me, to hold me, to walk me around, and he cried. He didn't want to see . . .'

'Oh!' I exclaimed. 'He didn't want to see?'

My mother looked at me, squinting a bit.

'No, he didn't want to see,' she said. Then she added:

'I think you all saw more than he did. You came out . . .'

I interrupted. 'We saw more than he did?'

And my mother: 'Yes, you others wanted to see . . . You came out of your room and stood next to him, but he wouldn't raise his eyes and you had yours wide open. You looked at him crying, at me trying to walk holding myself up on the furniture, and then I shouted at him to send you away, but he didn't even know how to do that. I would've liked to see my father in his place.'

'Your father?' I said.

'Absolutely!' my mother cried. 'He was a great man, a great horseman and a farmer who could hoe the ground eighteen hours a day, and he had courage, and he did everything himself when my mother gave birth . . . That's why I would have liked to see him in your father's place. I told him to send you away, and he didn't do a thing, he didn't understand, didn't raise his eyes, was afraid to look. And I called him a coward, told him to help me, to hold me because I was in pain, and you know what he told me? He said, "Wait until they come."'

'Who was coming?' I said.

'The women he'd gone to call . . . But the women didn't always arrive in time, and one time I felt the head of the baby outside me, it was my third child, and I threw myself on the bed and said to him, "Run, it's coming!"'

'And we were there watching?' I said.

And my mother: 'Of course . . . He hadn't sent you away. But you were very small, it was just you and Felice, you two and a half, Felice around a year old or a little more, the baby was the third . . . I saw that he had his head all outside . . .'

'And we were there watching?' I said.

And my mother: 'Yes! And even the baby was there watching, with all his head outside and his eyes open, he was a beautiful baby, and I shouted at your father to run and pull him out. And do you know what he did? He lifted his arms to the sky and began to invoke God just as when he recited his tragedies . . .'

'Oh!' I said.

And my mother: 'Yes, that's what he did . . . And the baby was getting purple in the face as he watched me, he was a beautiful baby, and I didn't want him to be strangled . . .'

'Then someone came . . .' I said.

And my mother: 'No! It was two in the morning and no one came . . . But I grabbed the bottle of water that was on the commode, I was really angry, and I threw it at your father's head . . .'

'You hit him?' I said.

And my mother: 'By God, I have a good aim! I hit him and that's how I got him to help me. And he helped, he pulled the baby out of me safe and sound as if he were another man and not himself, but of course it was more my pushing than his pulling, his face was all blood and sweat . . .'

'See, he wasn't a coward,' I said. 'He didn't lack courage. He just had something else in him too, which went away when he saw the blood.'

'What something else?' my mother exclaimed, and gazed into the now empty plate. 'What else could he have had? He wasn't a man like my father!'

Then she got up from the table, and went into a dark room behind the kitchen, maybe a pantry, and it was curious how lightly she walked in her big shoes.

XV

'Where are you going?' I called out behind her.

Her voice came back to me muffled, as if under a shawl of dust. 'I'm getting a melon.' And I was sure that in the back there was an unused room with a low roof, a storage space.

I waited, and there was no more herring on the plate, nor scent of herring in the kitchen. And my mother came back, carrying a long melon in one hand. 'See, sweetheart?' she said. 'A winter melon!'

She smiled, and she was like an apparition, twice real with the melon in her hand; she herself, and my childhood memory of her back in the plate-layers' houses.

'We used to have winter melon,' I said.

And my mother: 'Yes. We used to keep them under

the straw in the chicken coop. Now I keep them here in the attic. I have a dozen of them.'

'We kept them in the chicken coop?' I said. 'It was a real mystery where you kept them! We never found out. It seemed as if you hid them inside you. And every once in a while, on a Sunday, you brought one out. You went away like you did just now and you came back with a melon . . . It was a mystery.'

And my mother: 'You must have looked everywhere.'

And I: 'We did! If they'd been in the chicken coop we would've found them.'

And my mother: 'But they were there. In a hole dug in the ground with straw over them.'

'Oh, I see!' I said. 'And we thought you hid them inside you, somehow.'

My mother smiled.

'Was that why you called me Mother Melon?' she said.

And I: 'We called you Mother Melon?'

And my mother: 'Or maybe Mother of the Melons . . . Don't you remember?'

'Mother of the Melons!' I exclaimed.

The melon was put on the table and rolled slowly towards me, once, twice, its strong green rind subtly streaked with gold. I bent over to smell it.

'That's it,' I said.

And there was a strong smell not only of the melon but an old smell like wine, the smell of lonely winters in the mountains, along the solitary track, and of the little dining room, with its low roof, in the plate-layer's house.

I looked around.

'There's none of our furniture here?' I said.

And my mother: 'None of the furniture. There are some pots and kitchen things of ours . . . And the bedspreads, the linens. The furniture we sold when we came here . . .'

'But what made you decide to come here?' I said.

And my mother: 'I decided. This is my father's house and there's no rent to pay. He built it himself, a piece of it every Sunday. Where else would you have me go?'

And I: 'I don't know. But it's so far from the train here! How can you live without even seeing the tracks?'

And my mother: 'What do I care about seeing the tracks?'

And I: 'I mean . . . without ever hearing a train pass!'

And my mother: 'What do I care about hearing a train pass?'

And I: 'I would've thought you cared . . . Didn't you used to go out to stand at the crossing with the little flag when it passed?'

'Yes, if I was not seeing one of you off,' my mother said.

And I exclaimed: 'Oh! Sometimes you would see us off?'

But it didn't matter to me how she might respond. I could remember having a special rapport, like a dialogue, with the train, as if I had spoken with it; and for a moment I felt as if I were trying to remember the things it told me, as if I were thinking about the world in the way I had learned from the train in our talks.

I said: 'There was a place where we lived near the station. Serradifalco, I think . . . We couldn't see the station, but we could hear the freight cars crashing against each other when they shunted them around . . .'

I remembered the winter, the great loneliness of the barren countryside, without trees or leaves, and the earth which smelled, in the winter, like a melon; and that noise.

'I loved to hear that noise!' I said.

'Cut the melon!' my mother cried.

I cut into the strong rind and the knife immediately sank in. My mother had meanwhile brought wine and glasses. And the wine wasn't very good, but the melon was open in the middle of the table and we drank its winter perfume.

XVI

Then I said: 'So?'

'So?' my mother asked.

'Yes, so?' I said. 'So what happened with Papa?'

My mother seemed irritated again.

'Why talk about it?' she grumbled. 'For me it's all the

same with him or without him . . . And if for him it's all the same without me, it doesn't matter to me.'

'So it's true that he took off with another woman?' I said.

And my mother: 'Took off? Oh no! I kicked him out. It's my house.'

And I: 'Oh dear! You got bored with him and kicked him out?'

And my mother: 'Yes. I put up with him for many years, but this was too much, I couldn't stand seeing him in love at his age . . .'

'How did he fall in love?'

And my mother: 'It was always that way with women. He always needed other women in the house and to play the cock-of-the-walk among the women . . . You know he wrote poetry. He wrote it for them . . .'

'There's nothing wrong with that,' I said.

And my mother: 'Nothing wrong with that? And them looking down on me after hearing themselves called queens in his poetry, there's nothing wrong with that?'

'He called them queens?' I said.

And my mother: 'Oh, yes. And even queen-bees! Those dirty wives of linekeepers and teachers, and stationmasters' wives . . . Queen-bees!'

And I: 'But how could they know he was referring to them?'

And my mother: 'Well! When one saw that he was nice to her, and at parties made toasts to the most beautiful woman while looking at her, and then read this poetry with his arms open towards her, what more did she need to know?'

I laughed. 'Oh, those parties! Those get-togethers!'

'He was a crazy man,' my mother said. 'He couldn't go without chatter and noise . . . Every six or seven days he simply had to get something together. He had to call the railway workers of the whole line together with their wives and daughters, so he could play the cock-of-the-walk among them all. There were times when he had get-togethers every night, at our house or at others' . . . Or a dance, or a card game, or a reading . . . And him the centre of attention, his eyes all lit up . . .'

I could remember my father with his blue eyes lit up, the centre of my childhood and of Sicily, in those lonely places in the mountains, and I remembered my mother, not unhappy really, playing the hostess and taking wine round and glowing, laughing, not at all unhappy to have such a cock-of-the-walk for a husband.

'He was good at that,' my mother continued. 'He never got tired of dancing and never missed a turn. Whenever a record finished, he ran to change it, came back, grabbed a woman and danced. And he knew how to lead a quadrille making funny jokes all the while . . . And he knew how to play the accordion and even the bagpipe. He was the best bagpipe player in all the mountains and he had a great voice that could fill up a valley. Oh! He was a great man, like an ancient warrior . . . And you could see that he felt like a king on his horse. And when the cavalcade appeared on the bridge, with the lanterns and bells, and him feeling like a king at the head, we shouted hooray! Long live Papa! we shouted.'

'But who are you talking about?' I asked.

'I'm talking about my father, your grandfather,' my mother said. 'Who do you think I'm talking about?'

And I: 'You're talking about Grandpa? It was Grandpa who played the record player?'

And my mother: 'No, that . . . that was your father. He played the record player and changed the records. He would run and change records the whole time. And he would dance the whole time. He was a great dancer, a great gentleman . . . And when he took me for a partner and made me spin around I felt like a girl again.'

'You felt like a girl with Papa?' I said.

And my mother: 'No! I mean with Papa, your grandfather . . . He was so tall and big, and so proud, with his white and blond beard!'

And I: 'So it was Grandpa who danced.'

And my mother: 'Your father danced, too. To the record player, with all those women he brought into my house . . . He danced too much. He wanted to dance every night. And when I didn't want to go to some party at a plate-layer's house that was too far away, he looked at me as if I'd taken away a year of his life. But we always wanted to go to the parties where he went . . .'

'He who?' I said. 'Papa or Grandpa?'

And my mother: 'Grandpa, Grandpa . . .'

XVII

My mother talked and talked a bit about Grandpa, or Papa, or about others there may have been, about men in general, and I found myself thinking he must have been a kind of Big Lombard.

I remembered nothing about my grandfather, only his holding me by the hand when I was three, or maybe five, taking me down the street or up the stairs of this house, his own spot on earth. But I could think of him as a sort of Big Lombard, like the big hairy fellow from the train, the one with the little white beard who had spoken of his horse and his daughters and of other duties.

'I guess he was a Big Lombard,' I said.

We had finished eating the melon, and my mother got up, gathering the plates. 'What's a Big Lombard?' she said.

I shrugged my shoulders. I didn't really know what to say. I said: 'A man . . .'

'A man?' my mother said.

And I: 'A tall, big man . . . Wasn't Grandpa tall?'

And my mother: 'He was tall. A tall man is called a Big Lombard?'

And I: 'Not really. Not for his height . . .'

And my mother: 'Then why do you think he was a Big Lombard?'

And I: 'Just because! Wasn't Grandpa blond with blue eyes?'

'And that makes him a Big Lombard? Someone blond with blue eyes? It doesn't take much to be a Big Lombard!'

'Okay,' I said. 'Maybe it doesn't take much, maybe it does . . .'

My mother had planted herself firmly in front of the table, her arms crossed over her old breasts, squinting a bit as she looked at me, wrapped in her red shawl.

'It doesn't take much to be blond and have blue eyes,' she said.

'That's true,' I said. 'But a Big Lombard doesn't have to be blond.'

I was thinking of my blue-eyed father who was not blonde, and how I thought even he was a kind of Big Lombard, in *Macbeth* and in all the tragedies he used to recite on the railway trestles, for the railway workers and plate-layers, and I said: 'He might just have blue eyes.'

'And so?' my mother said.

And I thought about what the Big Lombard had actually been like, the man on the train who had spoken of other duties, and in my memory of him it seemed he didn't have blue eyes, that he was only a man with a lot of hair.

'Okay,' I said. 'A Big Lombard has a lot of hair. Did Grandpa have a lot of hair?'

'A lot of hair?' my mother said. 'No, not a lot. He had a big beard, white and blond . . . But he was balding in the middle of his head . . . He wasn't a Big Lombard!'

'Oh yes!' I said. 'He was a Big Lombard all the same.'

And my mother. 'How could he be, if you say a Big Lombard has a lot of hair? He didn't have a lot of hair . . .'

And I: 'What difference does hair make? I'm sure Grandpa was a Big Lombard . . . He must have been born in a Lombard town.'

'In a Lombard town?' my mother exclaimed. 'What's a Lombard town?'

And I: 'A Lombard town is a town like Nicosia. Do you know Nicosia?'

And my mother: 'I've heard of it. It's where they make bread with hazelnuts on top . . . But my father wasn't from Nicosia.'

'There're lots of other Lombard towns,' I said. 'There's Sperlinga, there's Troina . . . All the towns in Val Demone were settled by Lombards.'

And my mother: 'Is Aidone a Lombard town? I once had an oil jug from Aidone. But he wasn't from Aidone.'

'Where's that?' I asked. 'I thought it was in Valle Armerina . . . Around there . . . There's also a Lombard town in Valle Armerina.'

'He was from Piazza,' my mother said. 'He was born in Piazza and then he came here. Is Piazza Armerina a Lombard town?'

I kept quiet and thought a moment, then said: 'No, I don't think Piazza is a Lombard town.'

And my mother was triumphant. 'See, he wasn't a Big Lombard.'

'I'm sure he was!' I exclaimed. 'He must have been.'

And my mother: 'But he wasn't from a Lombard town!'

And I: 'What difference does it make where he was from? Even if he'd been born in China I'm sure he would have been a Big Lombard.'

Then my mother laughed. 'You're stubborn!' she said. 'Why do you want so much for him to be a Big Lombard?'

And I laughed, too, for a moment. Then I said: 'The way you talk about him, it seems he must have been. It seems he must have thought about other duties . . .'

This I said more seriously, longing for the Big Lombard I met on the train, and for men like him – my father in *Macbeth*, my grandfather, and men like him, made in his image. 'It seems he must have thought about other duties,' I said.

'Other duties?' my mother said.

And I: 'Didn't he ever say that the duties we have now are old ones? That they're decayed, dead, and it no longer satisfies us to fulfil them?'

My mother was disconcerted. 'I don't know. I don't think so,' she said.

And I: 'He didn't say that we need other duties? New duties, not the usual ones? He didn't say that?'

'I don't know,' my mother said. 'I don't know. I didn't hear him say it . . .'

Now, once again, it seemed it didn't matter to me that I was there, at my mother's, on this journey, instead of in my everyday life. Nevertheless, still longing for the Big Lombard, I asked: 'Was he satisfied with himself? Was he satisfied with himself, and the world, Grandpa?'

My mother looked at me a bit, disconcerted, and was about to say something. But she changed her mind and said: 'Why not?' Then she looked at me again, and I didn't respond, and she kept on looking at me, and once again changed her mind, and said: 'No, deep down he wasn't.'

'He wasn't?' I said.

And my mother: 'No, he wasn't, not with the world.'

'And with himself he was?' I said. 'He wasn't satisfied with the world but with himself he was?'

And my mother: 'Yes, with himself I believe he was.'

'He was?' I said. 'He didn't think about other duties?'

And my mother: 'Why shouldn't he have been satisfied? He felt like a king on his horse, in the cavalcade . . . And he had us, three beautiful daughters! Why shouldn't he have been?'

And I: 'Okay. Maybe you don't know whether he was or wasn't . . .'

XVIII

Then my mother set about doing the dishes. There was no running water and she washed them in a terracotta basin full of warm water, and as she washed she suddenly began to whistle.

'Can you help me?' she said when she pulled the first plate from the warm water. I got up to help her. She scrubbed the plate with a bit of ash, and passed it to me, pointing out a bucket of cold water; she wanted me to rinse each plate in the bucket, then dry it. We continued this way with the other plates and cutlery, while she whistled and sang, and I watched her.

She sang, I say, but under her breath, old tunes without words, in a half moan, half whistle, and warble all at once, and she was a funny lady of fifty or a little less, with her face still not old (dried up by the years, but not old – actually young) and with her nearly blond chestnut-brown hair, with the red shawl over her shoulders, with Papa's shoes on her feet. I saw her hands, and they were big, gnarled, used-up hands, completely different from her face because they could also be the hands of a man who chopped down trees or worked the ground, while her face, somehow, was that of an odalisque.

'These women of ours!' I thought, and I meant not Sicilian women but women in general without gentle, bedroom hands. Maybe they were unhappy about that, wildly jealous for that reason, not having the hands of odalisques to match their hearts and faces, not being able to keep their men tied to them with their hands. I thought of my father and myself, all men, with our need for soft hands touching us, and I thought I understood something of our uneasiness with women; of our readiness to desert them, our women with their rough, almost masculine hands, their tough hands in bed at night; and of how like slaves we would submit to calling a woman a queen who was a woman, an odalisque, when she touched us. That was why, I thought, we loved the idea of people living in luxury, the idea of the whole civil–military society and of the hierarchies, the dynasties, and the princes and kings in the fables – because of the idea of the woman who cultivated her hands for tenderness. It was enough to know that she existed, to be able to know that there were such women, and to see them, here and there, with their horses and eunuchs and coats-of-arms; and this was why, I thought, we loved all the celebrations and the great harems, we even loved their men and the trumpets and the coats-of-arms, and this was why we took our eyes off the women and children who were our equals and continued to play the field, looking for other women – myself, my father, all men, looking for something else in those other women without ever knowing that we were hoping to be touched by tender hands. That's what I thought, and I thought we were cowards, as I looked at the shapeless hands of my mother and thought of her shapeless feet in the old men's shoes, which one had to overlook as unmentionable parts of another nature in her. But my mother was singing and she was a bird singing in a moan, whistle and warble all at once, and her hands and her feet didn't matter, and even her age didn't matter, it mattered only that she sang, a bird, the mother-bird of the air and the light, laying eggs of light. 'Okay,' I said, 'I imagine you spending your time like this when you're alone.'

'Like this?' my mother said.

'Yes,' I said. 'Singing.'

My mother shrugged, as if she might not have known she was singing. And I added: 'It doesn't bother you to be alone?'

Then she looked at me, squinting as she did when perplexed. Then she wrinkled her brow, saying: 'If you think I miss your father's company you're fooling yourself . . . What makes you think such things?'

'Why?' I said. 'Wasn't he good company? He also helped you do the dishes, I bet.'

And my mother: 'That doesn't mean I have to feel lonely without him . . .'

And I: 'But he was a nice man!'

And my mother: 'Oh! One shouldn't have a nice man in the house! That was my bad luck, that he was a nice man . . .'

And I: 'I wish you would explain yourself better.'

And my mother: 'Well, your grandfather wasn't nice . . .

He never called women queens, he never wrote them poetry . . .'

'He didn't like women, I suppose,' I said.

And my mother: 'He didn't like women? He liked them ten times better than your father . . . But he didn't need to call them queens. When he liked one he took her into the ravine. There are many here in town who still remember him. And many in Piazza, too . . .'

'And you're complaining about Papa?' I said. 'I think you would have been worse off, with your character, being the wife of someone like Grandpa.'

'Worse off?' my mother exclaimed. 'Worse off how?'

'Well,' I said. 'Grandpa took them into the ravine and Papa wrote them poetry. I have an idea that the ones sneaked into the ravine would have been harder on you than the poetry . . .'

And my mother: 'Not at all! All the trouble was in the poetry, with your father . . . I would have been happy if he'd only taken them into the ravine.'

And I: 'What? If he took them into the ravine and then wrote them poetry?'

And my mother: 'Of course. He called them queens, treated them like queens. He was a nice man. And if one of them had a nice name like Manon, for example, he seemed to go crazy, a ridiculous thing at his age.'

'Who had the name Manon?' I asked.

And my mother: 'That one was the horsewoman in the circus. I kicked him out over her . . . Because her name was Manon, he always treated her like a queen. He was a nice man.'

There was a pause in which my mother seemed to be waiting for me to respond. So I said: 'He was a nice man.'

And my mother: 'That was the trouble. I would have been happy if he'd only taken them into the ravine . . . Instead he would come and say to me: "My dear, if you were a little girl, your name could be Manon."'

'And that was the trouble?' I said.

'The trouble was that he treated them like queens, not like filthy cows. And he let them think who knows what. That was the trouble. I couldn't look down on them.'

'Oh!' I said. 'You couldn't look down on them?' And meanwhile I thought: what a strange woman!

And my mother said: 'He let them think they were who knows what and they looked at me as if I were who knows what . . . They came into my house, wives of railway workers, farmers, and they were bold, at ease, they didn't lower their eyes, they looked at me as if I were who knows what. And I couldn't look down on them!'

What a strange woman! I thought.

And my mother said: 'That was the trouble! He let them think they were much better than me! And they looked at me as if they were much better than me! Because he called them queens! He didn't let them think they were filthy cows. And I couldn't look down on them.'

That is how she talked and I thought: what a strange

woman! what a strange woman! and inside I was almost laughing. I knew how we men were, cowards maybe, my father and myself, but right, after all, in our enthusiasm for women and in letting them think they were who knows what, and inside I was almost laughing.

XIX

My mother had picked up a broom and was now sweeping around us, and she was both my mother and a woman, very richly so, and, almost laughing inside, I thought that even she might once have been one of those she called filthy cows; a queen for other men despite her red hands, in secret; and a queen bee, and a mother of passions.

Why not? I thought.

She had too much richness of a mother in her to have been just a wife letting herself waste away, pathetically, poor thing, because of her man's enthusiasm for other women. She had too much old honey in her, as she now moved about in this little kitchen, standing so tall, with her nearly blond hair, the red shawl over her shoulders. She had too much old honey in her. She could not have been just a poor thing.

And almost laughing inside, I said: 'You're a strange woman! Did you want them to feel like cows?'

'That's what I wanted,' my mother said. 'I wanted to be able to laugh about it.'

'Strange woman!' I said. 'You would have laughed about it?'

'Naturally. It wouldn't have meant anything to me! I would have laughed about it! But he didn't treat them like cows . . .'

'Why should he? Didn't they have husbands, like you, and even children, like you?'

'Okay! But no one made them act like cows.'

'Was what they did so filthy? Didn't they do the same thing you did with him? Or did they do something else?'

'What something else?' my mother exclaimed.

And for a moment she stopped sweeping.

'What do you mean, something else?' she said. 'They did the same thing, naturally. What else could they do?'

'Well, then?' I said. 'They had husbands, like you. They had children, like you. And they didn't do anything filthier than you and he did too . . . Why should he have treated them like filthy cows?'

'But he wasn't their husband, he was my husband . . .'

'That's the difference?' I said. And inside I was laughing. I looked at her standing nonplussed in the middle of the kitchen, the broom in her hand, no longer sweeping, and I laughed inside.

'I don't understand your reasoning,' I said. And, laughing inside, I decided to take the risk.

'I don't understand your reasoning,' I said again. 'Were you a filthy cow when you did it with other men?'

My mother didn't blush. Her eyes blazed, her lips became rigid, and her whole body went rigid as she straightened, standing taller, stirred up in her old honey, but she didn't blush.

And laughing inside, I said: 'Because I suspect even you went into the ravine . . .' I was happy to stir her up in her old honey and, laughing inside, I started to talk freely.

'You couldn't have always been in the kitchen!' I said. 'You could have been in the ravine with someone!'

'Oh!' my mother said. She stood like stone in the middle of the kitchen, beside herself in her old honey, but not blushing, not ashamed. 'Oh!' she said, looking down on me.

She was more than my mother as she said this, a mother-bird, mother-bee; but the old honey in her was too old and it calmed, settled in her, mischievously. I was after all only a twenty-nine-year-old son, nearly thirty, estranged from her for fifteen years, for half my life, the half in which I had become a man, and so she said, starting to sweep again, 'Well, I suppose he deserved it if I went with another man once or twice.'

I said, 'Of course he deserved it!'

Then I asked:

'Many times? With many men?'

'Oh!' my mother exclaimed. 'Do you think I pulled my wagon for their men?'

'No! I just wanted to know if it happened with one man or with two . . .'

'With one! With one! Because one other time it was a mistake and doesn't count.'

'A mistake?' I said. 'What do you mean, a mistake?'

'It happened with a friend when we were in Messina. After the earthquake . . . It was something that happened in the confusion, that's all. I was very young and we never spoke of it again.'

'You see!' I said. 'And with the other one?'

'Oh! With the other one it happened by chance!'

'Was he also a friend of ours?' I said.

'No. It was somebody I didn't know.'

'Someone you didn't know?' I exclaimed.

'What are you so surprised about? You don't know what happened.'

'I'm thinking that he raped you!'

'Raped?'

Inside I laughed at the tone in which my mother said this. Then, seeing her as if from another spot on earth, not from there in her own kitchen, in her Sicily, I asked: 'But where did it happen? Were we already living in one of the plate-layers' houses?'

XX

'We were living in Acquaviva,' my mother said.

I listened to her now from another spot on earth and imagined Acquaviva very far away in space, a lonely place at the foot of a mountain. Yet I said: 'But in Acquaviva we were all getting big. It was after the war.'

'So what?' my mother said. 'Did I have to ask your permission because you were getting big? You were eleven. You went to school and you went to play . . .'

That's how life was in those lonely places, Acquaviva, San Cataldo, Serradifalco, the children having left for school on a freight train, or playing in the nooks and crannies of the barren countryside, the man at work with a shovel, the mother at work with the wash or something else, everyone saddled with his own devil under the sky of lonely places.

It was glorious to be so far away in space, while my mother told me it had been a terrible summer. Not a trickle of water in all the streams for sixty miles in every direction and nothing in sight but stubble from where the sun rose to where it set. There were no houses for fifteen or twenty miles in every direction, except, along the tracks, the plate-layers' houses crushed to the ground with loneliness. That it was a terrible summer meant not a bit of shade for all those miles, cicadas burst open by the sun, snails dried out by the sun, everything in the world having turned into sun. 'It was a terrible summer,' my mother said.

She had finished sweeping, and moved about the kitchen putting various things in order, and she didn't tell the story so much as simply respond to my questions. 'Was it morning, or afternoon?' I asked.

'I think it was afternoon. There were no wasps, no flies, nothing . . . It must have been afternoon.'

'And what were you doing?' I asked.

'I had baked bread . . .'

So, for miles and miles the smell of dead snakes in the sun, then, suddenly, near a house, the smell of freshly baked bread. 'I had baked bread,' my mother said.

'And then?' I asked.

'I was washing. We had a basin outside, next to the well and it must have been afternoon because it was shady just where the basin was . . . I always washed in the afternoon.'

So it was afternoon, and there was the smell of freshly baked bread around a house, and water which had been brought by train in a water cistern, and a woman washing. But my mother didn't tell the story, she answered my questions. I asked: 'And so, what about him?'

'He was a vagrant.'

'A vagrant!' I exclaimed.

'Yes, travelling on foot,' my mother said.

And I: 'Across all those miles where there wasn't a trickle of water . . . where there were no towns?'

'Yes. Carrying a little rucksack of clothes and dressed in a soldier's uniform without the decorations, an old harvester's hat on his head. He had taken off his shoes and carried them tied together, over his shoulders . . .'

'Had he come from far away?'

'I imagine so . . . He told me that he had passed through Pietraperzia, Mazzarino, Butera, Terranova and a hundred other places. He seemed to have come directly from wherever the war had ended. He was still dressed like a soldier, though he didn't have the decorations.'

'All on foot?' I said. 'Through Terranova, Butera, Mazzarino, Pietraperzia?'

'On foot . . . He hadn't seen a town or a living soul in forty-eight hours.'

'And he hadn't eaten in forty-eight hours? He hadn't had anything to drink in forty-eight hours?'

'More, he said . . . The last place he'd passed had been a farm, and dogs keep vagrants away from farms. That's what he told me, while he drank a bucket of water.'

She stopped, as if she had nothing more to say, and I asked: 'Water was all he wanted?'

'He wanted something else if he could have it,' my mother said. 'He didn't ask, really, but I gave him a loaf of bread I'd baked not more than an hour before, dressed with oil, salt and oregano, and he sniffed the air, smelled the bread, and said, blessed be God!'

Again my mother stopped and wouldn't tell the story

but would only answer my questions, and I asked her something, I don't know what, and she said that while the man said blessed be God and ate the bread, he was looking at her. And again I asked her something, I don't know what, and my mother said she'd understood that the man was hungry and thirsty for something else, too, and didn't ask, saying blessed be God, but also wanted something else if he could have it. And again I asked her something, I don't know what, and my mother said that she had wanted the man not to be hungry and thirsty for anything, and had wanted to see him satisfied, that it seemed to her Christian and charitable to satisfy him even in his hunger and thirst for something else. And I thought, Blessed Cow! and said: 'But then even this was just something in passing!'

'No,' my mother said, 'the man came back other afternoons.'

'He was from that area, then? He wasn't a vagrant?'

'He was a vagrant. He was on his way to Palermo and he had crossed all of Sicily.'

'He was on his way to Palermo? He went on to Palermo?'

'He was on his way, but he didn't get there. He got as far as Bivona and found work in a sulphur mine, so he stopped there.'

'In Bivona?' I said. 'But Bivona is a long way from Acquaviva . . .'

'It's over the mountain. About thirty miles away . . . Other towns are all at least thirty miles from Acquaviva.'

'No,' I said. 'Casteltermini is closer than thirty miles. Why didn't he stop in Casteltermini?'

'Maybe there was no work in Casteltermini. Or maybe he wanted to continue towards Palermo, got to Bivona, and changed his mind.'

'And he came thirty miles on foot to visit you?' I said.

'Thirty coming and thirty returning. He was a vagrant . . . On the seventh day from that afternoon, he turned up again.'

'Did he turn up often?'

'A number of times. He brought me little presents. Once he brought me a honeycomb of fresh honey which perfumed the whole house . . .'

'Oh!' I exclaimed. And said: 'Why did he stop coming?'

'Well,' my mother said. And she was about to go on, but looked at me and asked: 'Aren't you going to ask me if he was a Big Lombard?'

'Oh!' I exclaimed. 'Why do you say that?'

'I believe he was,' my mother said. 'I believe he thought about other duties. Isn't a Big Lombard someone who thinks about other duties?'

'He thought about other duties?' I exclaimed. 'Him? The vagrant?'

'Yes,' my mother said. 'Towards winter there was a strike in the sulphur mines, and the farmers rebelled, too, trains came by loaded with royal guards . . .'

Now my mother was telling the story, I no longer had

to keep questioning her. 'The railway workers didn't strike,' she said. 'Trains loaded with royal guards passed. And more than a hundred died in Bivona; not the guards, the strikers . . .'

'And you think he was one of those who died?'

'I think so,' my mother said. 'Because otherwise, wouldn't he have turned up again?'

'Oh!' I said. And I looked at my mother, I saw that she had nothing more to do in the kitchen and that she was calm, tranquil. With her hand, she was smoothing her dress against her leg, and again I thought: Blessed Cow!

Part Three

XXI

There was doleful bleating outside in the afternoon, and it didn't fade away, it rose and became a music: bagpipes.

'The novenas are beginning now,' my mother said. Then she added: 'I have to make my rounds.' She sat down on a chair to change her shoes, took off the men's shoes and put on a pair of women's ankle boots which were under the table.

'Your rounds? What rounds?' I asked.

'I'll take you with me,' my mother said.

She got up, taller and wavering a bit in her ankle boots, and went into her bedroom to get dressed to go out. From there she talked to me while the bagpipe music went on. She said she had started giving injections. She said she didn't believe she could expect anything from my father, and she had started making her living this way, giving injections.

Dressed in a black overcoat, and with a big bag a little like a midwife's on her arm, she led me out into the cold sun, and my journey in Sicily began anew.

XXII

We passed behind the house on a street which went
downhill and, passing between garden walls, we came
to a door and knocked. The door opened.

Inside it was dark, and I couldn't see who had opened
it. There were no windows; there was only, high up in
the door, an opening with a blackish pane. I couldn't
see a thing, I couldn't even see my mother any longer.

I could hear her speak, though.

'I have my son with me,' she said.

Then she asked: 'How is your husband?'

'As usual, Concezione,' a woman's voice answered.

And exclaimed: 'What a big son you have!'

And from the back a man's voice spoke:

'I'm here in bed, Concezione.'

The man's voice sounded as though it came from underground, and spoke again: 'He's your son, this one?'

'This is Silvestro,' my mother said.

They were speaking far away from me, all three voices;
they were the voices of invisible creatures. They were
also talking about me.

'You made him big like you!' said the woman's voice.

They could see me and they were invisible: they were
like spirits. And like a spirit my mother gave the injection
perfectly in the dark, talking about ether and a needle.

'You must eat,' she said. 'Eat more and you'll get

better sooner. What have you eaten today?'

'I ate an onion,' the man's voice answered.

'It was a good onion,' the woman's voice said. 'I roasted it for him in the cinders.'

'Good,' my mother said. 'You should also give him an egg.'

'I gave him one on Sunday,' the woman's voice said.

And my mother said: 'Good.'

From deep in the darkness she yelled to me: 'We're going now, Silvestro.'

I was stroking the warm fur of a goat in front of me. I had moved a few steps forward on the uneven floor of bare earth and searching with my hands I had met warm animal fur, and had stayed still, in the cold dark, warming my hands on this living fur.

'We're going now,' my mother repeated.

But the voice of the man, from the back, held her another minute.

'How many more injections do I have to have?' it asked.

'The more you have, the better the cure,' my mother responded.

'I have five more to go, though,' the voice added.

And the voice of the wife said: 'Do you think with those five more he'll be cured?'

'Everything is possible,' my mother responded.

Then she opened the door, and my mother became visible again on the threshold, with her midwife's bag over her arm.

We went out and began walking again, between the walls of the gardens, towards another house on my mother's rounds. We turned onto a street which ran downhill below the first. Facing us across the open spaces of the valley was the mountain hairy with snow; and on one side of us, in their gardens, little houses rose against the sky and faraway mountain; on the other side, in wan sunlight, there were passages to homes carved into the rock beneath the huts and the gardens further up. The gardens were tiny; higher up, seen between the roofs, they seemed like planters full of greenery; and in the street there were goats sluggish in the sun; in the cold air, there was the bagpipe music and the tinkling of the goats' bells. It was a little Sicily heaped up with medlar trees and roofing tiles, of holes in the rock, of black earth, of goats, with bagpipe music which faded in the distance behind us and turned into clouds or snow, high up.

I asked my mother:

'What illness did that man have?'

'The same as all the others,' my mother said. 'Some have a little malaria. Some have a little TB.'

XXIII

We walked only a minute or two before my mother knocked at another door, and again I found myself in the dark, on a floor of bare, uneven earth. It smelled like an abandoned well.

'I have my son with me,' my mother said again.

And again I heard them talk about me, people I couldn't see, and among the voices I could pick out the small voice of a child.

My mother said: 'Do you have the little vials?'

'We've got them.' The voice of a man replying.

Other voices talked all at once.

'Light the fire, Teresa.'

'Get the straw.'

And the voice of the man talked with the voice of the child. It was the voice of a man holding his one- or two-year-old son in his arms. My mother said something more about the injection, and the man answered and made noises as he opened a drawer, accompanied by the small, high voice of his son in his arms.

Then, in that intense darkness like the interior of a well, the light of a match flared and I saw my mother's hands, and after that moment of light on her hands I heard her ask:

'All right?'

Two or three times she asked: 'All right?'

She asked: 'How do you feel?'

And the man's voice asked loudly together with hers:

'Concezione is asking how you feel.'

'Eh?' came the response.

And my mother asked:

'What have you given her to eat?'

'We gave her chicory tonight,' the man's voice answered.

Then there was the question about how many more injections were necessary, and we left those spirits, and went away. My mother said that it was lucky it was the woman who was sick instead of the man, because it doesn't matter if a woman is sick, but if a man gets sick, goodbye . . .

'What do you mean, goodbye?' I asked.

'They won't eat again, winter or summer,' my mother said.

And she said that in general women don't know what to do when the man gets sick; they don't even know how to go pick a little chicory in the valley, or even how to go look for snails on the plains; they don't know how to do anything but get into bed with the man.

XXIV

The music of the bagpipes was far away, at the highest point of the town, perfectly transformed into cloud or snow, and down below in the valley there now rose the roar of a stream.

We entered a suffocating darkness. It was all dark and smoke; yet the voices of the invisibles spoke calmly like those in the other houses. Even the voice of my mother spoke undisturbed by the smoke.

'I have my son with me,' she said.

She had the same discussion as before; she spoke of me, then of the little vials and the needle; and for a moment the light of a match flickered over her hands. When the light went out she asked:

'Well, then, how are you?'

The response was: 'Mah!'

And my mother asked:

'What have you given her to eat?'

'We'll be eating now' was the response.

And 'We're cooking.'

There were many voices.

So we went out again, and my mother said the opposite of what she had said before. She said it was bad luck when a woman was sick, the mother. It was better when the man was sick, she said. So many men didn't work in the winter anyway, and were good for nothing, and if the woman got sick, goodbye . . . Because a woman, she said, could always go to pick chicory in the valley or to look for snails on the plain. It was the woman, the mother, who kept the household going.

And again we entered a darkness, again my mother became invisible, spoke invisibly.

She spoke of me: 'I have my son with me!'

Then she spoke of the little vials and the needle, and gave the injection while for a moment the flame of a match lit up her hands. Then she asked if the sick one had eaten, and

they told her what he had eaten that evening or would eat
tomorrow, and we went out, my mother became visible
again and said the opposite of what she had said before,
said that when a man was sick, goodbye . . .

And again we descended through the black ditch of
the street, where there was no more sunlight, where
everything was in shadow, with the tinkling of the bells
of the goats and the noise of the stream, in the cold;
and again we entered dark places smelling like wells,
darkness and the smell of darkness, and darkness and
smoke, and my mother talking about me as a preamble,
speaking of the little vials and the needles, putting forth
questions about their eating; and always, while we were
leaving, there was a little suspense in a worried voice
wanting to know how many more injections one had to
have in order to be cured, and if one had to have more
than a certain number like five or seven or ten.

In this way we journeyed through little Sicily heaped
up with medlar trees and slate; with the noise of streams
outside, and of spirits inside, in the cold and dark;
and my mother was a strange creature who seemed to
live with me in the light and with those others in the
shadows, without ever getting lost the way that I got a
little lost every time we went in or out.

Every time we went out, she said the opposite of
what she'd said the time before. One time she would
say that when the man was sick, goodbye . . . and the
next time she would say that when the woman was sick,
goodbye . . .

She would say: 'Some have a bit of TB, some have a bit of malaria.'

And one time she would say it was better to have a bit of malaria than a bit of TB; the next time she would say it was better to have a bit of TB than a bit of malaria. She would say:

'With malaria you don't have to go to Enna for the medication.'

She told me it was a disaster to have to go to Enna to get TB medication from the dispensary, to have to make a long trip, to have to spend 32 lire, and then run the risk of being stuck in the hospital. People went to Enna the first time, she told me, then they didn't want to go there again. They couldn't afford it.

'The town gives out malaria medication,' she said.

But the next time she would say:

'With TB, you just have to go Enna and they have all the medication you want.'

She told me it was a disaster to have to depend on the town for malaria medication. The town was poor, it didn't have much medicine, and it never gave out more than one box. How could one get well on one box?

'The dispensary in Enna gives out the TB medicine,' she said. 'It's big, it's rich, it's supported by the government,' she said.

And each time she said the opposite of what she'd said the time before.

XXV

Now very close to the roar of the stream, we entered a house where there was light.

It was not a house carved from the rock, it was a stone house rising from a garden at the edge of the street. It had, at the back, a window, and from this window a bit of light.

'Good evening, I have my son with me,' my mother said as she entered.

This time she didn't become invisible and I could see people, could see in them all the people I hadn't been able to see earlier. I saw the sick man on the bed, with his eyes closed in a face dirty with beard; and I saw five or six women, probably sisters, sitting at the foot of the bed around a bucket placed on the ground.

As usual, my mother spoke of me first.

'I have my son with me,' she said.

Now I could see how she said it and how I was looked at by the others when she spoke.

'You have a big son!' one said.

'Mine are all big and this one is the biggest,' my mother said.

And the woman asked:

'Where has he been?'

My mother and the women talked about me, as usual, and I saw that the women had filled the bucket with black snails and were taking snails one at a time and sucking them. The women were young and old, dressed in black, and when they had finished sucking they threw the shells back in the bucket.

'*Buon appetito!*' my mother said.

She then began to talk about the little vials, the needle, the ether; she opened her bag, turned towards the sick man and gave him the injection.

I saw the sick man remain flat on his face.

'All right?'

This time an old woman responded.

'It's no use . . . He won't talk.'

'He won't talk?' my mother exclaimed.

'He won't talk,' another of the women responded.

The five women sitting at the foot of the bed kept sucking, and the eldest said loudly:

'Gaetano, say something. It's Concezione.'

Slowly the sick man turned over on his side, but he didn't respond. The eldest of the women turned to my mother:

'See? He doesn't want to talk,' she said.

My mother bent over the sick man; I saw her put a hand on his shoulder.

'What's this all about, Gaetano!' she said. 'You don't want to talk?'

Slowly the sick man turned from his side onto his back, revealing his face, but again he didn't respond. Nor had he opened his eyes.

'It's no use, Concezione,' said the eldest of the women.

'He doesn't want to talk ... He didn't talk all day yesterday.'

My mother asked:

'Has he eaten?'

The women pointed to the bucket and the eldest responded:

'Yes, he ate.'

Then the sick man suddenly spoke. He cursed.

I looked at him and saw that his eyes were open. He had fixed them on me, examining me, and I examined him, looking him in the eye, and for a moment it was as if we were alone, man to man, beyond even the circumstance of illness. I didn't even see the colour of his eyes, I saw in them only that they were human.

'Where did you come from?' he said.

'I'm Concezione's son,' I said.

The man closed his eyes again and my mother said to the women:

'You should try to keep him cheerful.'

Then to me:

'Silvestro, we're going.'

XXVI

I had been very sick, for months, some time before, and I understood the profundity of it, the profound misery of working-class human misery, especially when you've already been in bed for twenty days, or thirty, and you're stuck there, surrounded by four walls, the bed-clothes, the metal kitchenware, and the wood of the chairs, the tables, the wardrobe.

Then there is nothing else in the world, and you look at these pieces of furniture, but can't do anything with them; you can't make soup out of a chair or a wardrobe. But the wardrobe is so big, it would provide enough to eat for a month! And you keep looking at those things as though they were things to eat; and maybe that's why the children become dangerous and break things, break things . . .

All day the littlest has a leg of the chair in his mouth and howls if his mother tries to take it away. She, the mother, the wife, that is, or rather the girlfriend, looks at books and every once in a while even takes one, sits down to read it. She spends hours flipping the pages and reading. And the sick man asks:

'What are you reading?'

The woman doesn't know what she's reading, but a book can be anything, a dictionary or an old grammar book. Then the sick man says:

'So now you decide to give yourself an education?'

And the woman puts the book back, but then keeps looking at the row of them, of books, not anything one can eat, and again she takes one, and this time she goes out of the house, stays out part of the afternoon.

'How much did you sell it for?' the sick man asks when she returns.

The woman says that she has sold it for one-fifty and the sick man is dissatisfied, he never really understands the situation, he has an incessant fever in the old bed day after day, lying on his side. Still he wants something, besides that book which was his ever since he was a boy, he's waiting for a bit of broth, and in the end he yells at his wife, who has bought bread and cheese instead for herself and the children.

'Hawks,' he says of his children.

At school, they have a bowl of soup every day. This is a good idea, to give a bowl of soup at school every day to the children of people who are dying of hunger. But it is only an appetiser. After that spoonful of soup the children come home ravenous, and they don't listen to reason, they want to eat at all costs, and they're like wild animals, they devour the legs of the chairs, they would like to devour their father and mother. If one day they were to find the sick man alone they would devour him. The medicines are on the night table, at the bedside. The children come from school, ravenous, their teeth sharpened, their hunger whetted, and they approach the sick man, they want to eat him, they are coming on wolf-feet . . . But their mother is at home, and the children leave the sick man alone and pounce on the medicines.

'Hawks,' the sick man says.

And meanwhile the gas man has cut off the gas, the electric man has cut off the lights, they spend the long nights in the dark in the sick man's room. Only the water hasn't been cut off; the water man comes every six months, so there's no immediate danger of his coming and cutting off the water, and they drink, and drink, and drink more water than it's possible to drink, cooked in every way and even raw.

But there is the landlady who comes every day, she wants to see 'Mister Sick', she wants to look him in the eye, and when she comes in and sees him she says:

'Well, Mister Sick, how luxurious to stay in bed and pay no rent ... Send your wife to wash my dishes at least.'

And the wife goes to the landlady's to wash the dishes, wash the floors, wash the clothes, all in place of the unpaid rent; and the sick man stays alone in the house those long hours with the incessant fever beating him in the face, beating him, beating him, pummelling him as if taking advantage of his solitude.

The wife comes back and the sick man asks her whether she's brought anything from the landlady.

'Nothing,' his wife says.

She never brings anything.

'But why don't you at least go and pick wild greens?'

His wife says: 'Where?'

She goes along the street and comes to the park; there's grass in the fields, there's green on the trees, that's greenery, and she plucks grass, she plucks fronds from fir trees and pines, then she even goes to the gardens and plucks flowers and returns with the greenery, leaves and flowers hidden at her breast. She throws it all on top of the sick man and he is a man among the flowers.

'Here,' his wife says. 'Greens!'

XXVII

I understood this and more. I could understand the misery of a sick man and of those around him, in the working class of humanity. And doesn't everyone understand it? Can't everyone understand it? Everyone is sick at some point, in the middle of life, and knows the stranger that is illness, and one's powerlessness over this stranger inside; or can understand one's fellow man . . .

But perhaps not every man is a man; and not all humanity is humanity. This is a doubt which arrives in the rain when you have holes in your shoes, water seeping through the holes in your shoes, and you no longer have anyone in particular dear to your heart, you no longer have your own particular life, you've done nothing and have nothing still to do, nothing even to fear, nothing more to lose, and you see, outside yourself, the world's massacres. One man laughs and another man cries. Both are men; even the laughing man has been sick, is sick; nevertheless he laughs *because* the other man cries. He is the one able to massacre, to persecute; the one who, in hopelessness, you see laughing over his newspapers and the ad posters for the newspapers; he doesn't belong with the one who laughs but also cries, in his calm, with someone else crying. So not every man is a man. One persecutes and another is persecuted; and not all humanity is humanity, only those who are persecuted. You can kill a man and he will be all the more a man. And so a sick man, a starving man, is all the more a man; and humanity dying of hunger is humanity all the more.

I asked my mother: 'What do you think?'

'About what?' my mother said.

'About all these people you give injections to.'

'I think that maybe they won't be able to pay me.'

'Okay,' I said. 'But every day you go to them anyway, you give them the injections, and you hope that this time, somehow they might be able to pay you. But what do you think about them? What do you think they are?'

'I don't hope,' my mother said. 'I know some can pay and some can't. I don't hope.'

'Still, you go to all of them,' I said. 'But what do you think about them?'

'Oh!' my mother exclaimed. 'If I go to one I can also go to another,' she said. 'It doesn't cost me anything.'

'But what do you think about them? What do you think they are?' I asked.

My mother stopped in the middle of the street where we were and turned a slightly squinted eye towards me. She also smiled, and said:

'What strange questions you ask! What should I think

about them? They are poor people with a little TB or a little malaria . . .'

I shook my head. My mother could tell that I was asking strange questions, but she wouldn't give me strange answers. And that was what I wanted, strange answers. I asked: 'Have you ever seen a Chinaman?'

'Certainly,' my mother said. 'I've seen two or three . . . They come by to sell necklaces.'

'Okay,' I said. 'When you have in front of you a Chinaman and you look at him and you see that he doesn't have a coat in the cold, and he has torn clothing and holes in his shoes, what do you think of him?'

'Oh! Nothing special,' my mother answered. 'We see plenty of people around here who don't have coats in the cold and have torn clothes and holes in their shoes . . .'

'Okay,' I said. 'But he's Chinese, he doesn't know our language and can't talk to anybody, can never laugh with anybody, is travelling among us with his necklaces and ties, with his belts, and he has no bread, no money, he never sells anything, he has no hope. What would you think of him when you saw him, such a poor, hopeless Chinaman?'

'Oh!' my mother answered. 'I see plenty of people like that, around here . . . Poor, hopeless Sicilians.'

'I know,' I said. 'But he's Chinese. He has yellow skin, slanted eyes, a flat nose, cheekbones sticking out and maybe he stinks. He is even more hopeless than all the others. He can't have anything. What would you think of him?'

'Oh!' my mother responded. 'Plenty of others who are not poor Chinese have yellow skin, flat noses and maybe stink. They're not poor Chinese, they're poor Sicilians, and still they can't have anything.'

'But look,' I said. 'He is a poor Chinaman who finds himself in Sicily, not in China, and he can't even talk about the weather with a woman. A poor Sicilian, meanwhile, can . . .'

'Why can't a poor Chinaman?' my mother asked.

'Okay,' I said. 'I imagine a woman wouldn't give anything to a poor vagrant who was Chinese instead of Sicilian.'

My mother frowned.

'I wouldn't know,' she said.

'You see?' I exclaimed. 'A poor Chinaman is poorer than all the others. What do you think of him?'

My mother was peeved.

'To the devil with the Chinese,' she said.

And I exclaimed: 'See? He is poorer than all the poor and you tell him to go to the devil. And when you have told him to go to the devil, and then you think of him, so poor in the world, hopeless and sent to the devil, doesn't it seem to you that he is more of a man, more a part of humanity than everyone else?'

My mother looked at me, still peeved.

'The Chinaman?' she said.

'The Chinaman,' I said. 'Or even the poor Sicilian who is sick in bed like those you injected. Isn't he more human, more a part of humanity?'

'Him?' my mother said.

'Him,' I said.

And my mother asked: 'More than who?'

'More than everyone else. He who is sick . . . suffers.'

'He suffers?' my mother exclaimed. 'That's the sickness.'

'That's all?' I said.

'Take away the illness and it's gone,' my mother said. 'It's nothing . . . It's the sickness.'

Then I asked:

'And when he is hungry and suffers, what's that?'

'Hunger,' my mother answered.

'That's all?' I said.

'What else?' my mother said. 'Give him something to eat and it's gone. It's the hunger.'

I shook my head. I couldn't get strange answers from my mother, but still I asked once again:

'And the Chinaman?'

Now my mother wouldn't give me any answer at all, strange or not strange; she shrugged her shoulders. She was right, of course; take away the sickness of the sick person, and he no longer suffers; give the hungry person something to eat and he no longer suffers. But humanity, in sickness, what is it? And what is it in hunger?

Isn't hunger all the suffering in the world become hunger? Isn't a hungry man all the more of man? Isn't he more a part of humanity? And the Chinaman?

XXVIII

Now we were no longer descending the hill of houses, we were climbing another side of it, from the bottom of the ravine we were heading towards the sunlight and the music of the bagpipes, high up like clouds or snow.

'Have you ever been sick?' I asked my mother.

'Once,' my mother said.

'What was it?' I asked.

'I don't know,' my mother answered. 'I didn't want to see a doctor and I don't know what it was . . . I got better on my own.'

'You got better on your own?' I said. 'You're always special . . .'

'Special?' my mother exclaimed. 'Special how?'

'I'm saying that maybe,' I answered, 'you think you're different from other people. Isn't that so?'

'I don't think anything,' my mother said.

And I asked:

'Was Papa ever sick?'

'Of course! He was like a baby. He had chills, a high temperature, one could tell it was malaria, but he wanted the doctor anyway . . .'

'Papa was a humble man.'

'He was afraid.'

'He was a humble man.'

I was a little tired, the road was uphill, with a low wall

on one side, and I leaned on the wall. I had journeyed away from being calm in my hopelessness, and I was journeying still, and the journey was also a conversation, it was present, past, memory, and fantasy; for me, it wasn't life and yet it was motion, and I leaned on the wall and thought of my blue-eyed father when he was tired – not Macbeth, not a king.

Sick, he was burdened with all the world's suffering, and he accepted that he wasn't Macbeth, he called the doctor, he wanted to get better, he was like a baby.

Is a man more of a man when he's like a baby? He's humble, he admits his misery and cries out in his misery. Is he more a part of humanity?

'He was a humble man, deep down,' I said again.

I looked at my mother and pulled my hand back from the wall.

'And Grandpa was never sick?' I asked.

'He was very sick,' my mother answered.

'What?' I exclaimed. 'Even Grandpa?'

'Why not?' my mother said. 'He was about forty, I was only seven or eight.'

'He didn't want to see a doctor, I imagine,' I said.

'No,' my mother said. 'He got better on his own. Once the poor people's doctor came, but he didn't come back, Papa didn't want him.'

'There you go! He thought he was special.'

'What rubbish! He thought he wasn't sick.'

'There you go,' I said. 'He thought he was special, he

couldn't get sick, someone like him. He was a proud man!'

My mother straightened her back and stood proudly.

'Certainly. He was a proud man,' she said.

'And what was it?' I asked her. 'A little TB or a little malaria?'

'No!' my mother exclaimed. 'He was really sick. He died and then revived!'

No longer leaning on the wall but on my mother's arm, I thought about men; myself, Papa, Grandpa, humble men and proud men; and I thought about humanity and its pride in the midst of misery, and I was proud to be a son of man.

Some, certainly, were not men, and not all humanity was humanity. But it wasn't because he was humble that a man wasn't a man. Nor because he was proud.

A man could cry like a baby, in his misery, and still be all the more a man.

And he could deny his own misery, be proud, and still be all the more a man.

A proud man is a Big Lombard and thinks about other duties, when he is really a man. Because of this he is all the more a man. And because of this, perhaps, his sickness is death and resurrection.

'It was pneumonia,' my mother recalled. 'Or something like that. And he didn't want the doctor. He said he wasn't sick. He sent the poor people's doctor away. Bread is very expensive for the poor, he said. Every mouthful costs a day of work. And he sent the doctor away. We have to work, he said. And he continued to work his fourteen hours a day. Until one day he died and then revived.'

'He was a great man, Grandpa,' I said.

'He was a great man,' my mother said.

Now, further up on the path, we had come out of the shadow of the valley, we were back in the sun and my mother said:

'What do you think of my injections? I'm good at them, no?'

'Very good,' I said.

'You see,' my mother said, and she was triumphant, she was satisfied.

'You see?' she said. 'I can earn my own living.'

We were far away from the sound of the stream, we were in sunlight, facing the sun, which would soon be setting, and we could hear the snow or cloud of bagpipe music spreading over the highest reaches of the town.

'Now we're going to see the widow,' my mother said. 'She has some money. She pays in cash.'

XXIX

The widow was a woman of about forty, with good flesh on her bones, and she lived on the first floor, in an apartment of two or three big rooms with high ceilings.

'They call her the widow,' my mother said. 'But she's not really widowed. She was kept by an important gentleman . . .'

'Why does she need injections?'

'Because she's a lady,' my mother answered. 'Gentlemen have injections. And she got used to it with them. But she may also have a bit of TB.'

She was a pleasing woman, in every way, and she had good flesh on her bones. It seemed that she lived alone, in her big rooms; she came herself to let us in.

'I was waiting for you, Concezione,' she said. 'I knew that a son of yours had come to visit. Is this he?'

The apartment, from the door on, had a strong smell as if all autumn it had been fermenting must. This was the smell of city houses which weren't poor, in Sicily – stuffy, suffocating, not intoxicating, a smell which was a carnal partner of the dark.

The widow greeted us noisily, laughing, and she had a large bosom, and a voice rich from her big-breasted bosom, and dark eyes, dark hair.

'I suppose I did well to bring him,' my mother said. 'A good-looking son, no?'

'And tall and strong!' the widow said. 'Worthy of you, Concezione.'

And she laughed noisily and ushered us into her rooms, which smelled of must, like the doorway and the stairs, but also a little of cinnamon. They were old rooms, without much furniture, but with at least twenty tinted postcards on the walls. The rooms were rather dark because the balconies looked over a courtyard garden, facing north.

My mother continued to talk about me.

'How did you know he'd come to see me?' she said. 'I expect I'd have been in trouble if I hadn't brought him . . .'

'Oh,' the widow responded. 'I would have stayed curious about him.'

She wanted, of course, to offer us marsala and biscotti. From the table where she offered them, one could see the whole apartment, two or three big rooms with many doors, all thrown open, and a table in each room, and an immense bed with a red shawl in one of them.

'And so,' the widow said.

And she laughed noisily. She asked me some questions about Northern Italy, and asked my mother if she had taken me with her to all the houses on her rounds.

'Naturally,' my mother said. She was satisfied to have imposed me on so many houses; she'd wanted to show me how good she was at giving the injections, she added. And the widow laughed. She looked at me, a man, with her dark eyes. And in a voice rich from her big-breasted chest, she said:

'But with me, no, Concezione.'

'What do you mean, with you, no?' my mother said.

'With me you're not going to show him how good you are at giving the injection.'

'Why not?' my mother said.

And the widow laughed, saying:

'I won't allow myself to be injected in front of him.'

'Why not?' my mother said. She was armed with the will to impose me. 'Why not?' she said.

'Because it's not necessary, Concezione,' the widow responded. 'Here it's not necessary. There are so many rooms. He can wait without going out into the street.'

'But it's not that,' my mother said. 'I want him to see how it's done.'

'He's seen it enough times already,' the widow responded. 'It's not necessary for him to see it here, too.'

And turning to me, laughing, she said, 'Isn't that true, Mr Silvestro?'

'Yes, I suppose,' I said. But I liked being imposed on her.

'What do you mean, yes?' my mother then asked. 'Don't you want to see how I give an injection to the lady?'

'Oh, yes,' I responded.

'There you go,' my mother said. 'He wants to see.'

'But Concezione!' the widow exclaimed. 'I don't want him to see me.'

My mother laughed.

'But he's my son,' she said. 'It's the same as me seeing you . . .'

'But he's a young man,' the widow said.

And my mother said, 'Do you think he's never in his life seen women?'

The widow didn't say anything more. She laughed and

surrendered. And with a gesture towards me she said laughing:

'And him waiting there, the devil!'

She lay down on the bed, and my mother uncovered her.

'This is an outrage, Concezione,' she said from her pillow, laughing.

And my mother stuck the needle in her flesh with gusto, and then looked at me, victorious, and pointing to that flesh, said: 'See how shapely she is?'

The widow squirmed on her bed, laughing. 'Oh, Concezione!' she said.

'And she's almost forty,' my mother said.

I complimented her.

And the widow cried, 'Oh, Mr Silvestro!' She tensed, wanting to get up but my mother held her down, uncovering her even more.

'Wait, so he can see you well,' she said. And to me: 'Look, Silvestro!'

'But it's an outrage!' the widow said, and struggled, wanting to get up.

Finally my mother let her get up, and the widow, laughing and red in the face, said to me: 'You're quite a devil, Mr Silvestro.'

We parted cordially, and my mother and I went out into the street, into the bagpipe music and the sun, facing the sunset, and we laughed, and my mother said that the widow had protested so much because she had been a kept woman and felt she was in an awkward position.

'But she's a good woman,' she said. 'And shapely, no?' she added. She looked at me, winked at me, while we crossed the street.

'Oh, yes!' I said.

'And she has fresh skin,' my mother added.

'Oh, yes,' I said.

And my mother: 'She has one of the best complexions for her age here in town.'

And I: 'I would think so.'

And my mother: 'But there are women her age who look better than she does. I was in better shape than she is,' she said. 'And compared to her I don't think I've lost my figure, now that I'm fifty,' she said.

'Oh, no!' I said.

'I'm always in good shape, aren't I?' my mother said.

'Oh yes,' I said. 'You don't have a single white hair.'

'You should see how youthful I am underneath.'

And I: 'You can be proud of yourself.'

'Naturally,' my mother exclaimed. 'That's what I used to say to your father. You should be proud of a wife as youthful as I am at my age ... But he doesn't understand a thing about women. He talked about nothing in his poetry but slender hands and eyes and so on and so forth.'

'I imagine he felt that he couldn't talk about other things in his poetry,' I said.

'Okay, but he could have considered the rest before talking,' my mother said. 'He would have been proud of me if he had considered the rest. My father was so proud of me and his other daughters . . . He used to say that no girl had a backside as shapely as ours in all of Sicily . . . Oh, he was proud of me, my father!'

XXX

Higher up, facing the sunset, we had come to another doorway like the widow's, but smaller and less pretentious, with one of the knockers broken.

'Now we're going to see one of my friends,' my mother said.

'To give her an injection too?' I asked.

'Yes,' my mother responded. 'I want you to see how youthful she is, too. Maybe more so than the widow . . . And she's almost forty, too.'

'Is she a widow, too?' I asked. 'That is,' I asked, 'was she kept by a big shot, too?'

'Oh no!' my mother answered. 'She's a married woman. She has four children.'

We entered the foyer through a worm-eaten doorway, and there too, around the stairs, there was the old smell of must common to houses of the not-poor, in Sicily. But inside the house there was less than at the widow's; everything in the house was too old, the furniture, the floor tiles, the curtains, the bedcovers, everything was too old and dead, and one smelled dust more than anything else.

'Why are you giving her injections?' I asked. 'Is she sick?'

'No,' my mother said. 'She thinks she's a little anaemic.'

'Will she let you inject her in front of me?' I said.

'Why not?' my mother said.

'If she doesn't want it, don't insist,' I said.

'But she will,' my mother said.

A five-year-old child had opened the door for us. Two other children greeted us, one perhaps seven years old, and one about eight or nine, all with long hair and long aprons so one couldn't tell if they were boys or girls. 'Concezione! Concezione!' they shouted, and took us back and forth through the house, where all the rooms were very dark, and then out onto a little terrace where we met a girl of sixteen or seventeen who also began to cry out, 'Concezione! Concezione!'

Finally we met my mother's friend.

'Concezione! Concezione!' she said.

She was not a very big woman, and in fact had nothing anaemic about her appearance, but was young, round and pleasing, with a lovely body. She threw herself on my mother and kissed her, with her arms round her neck, as if she had not seen her for months, and while the children jumped up and down and shouted, she said, 'I heard you'd be bringing your son!'

'You knew he'd come to visit me?' my mother said.

'Yes,' my mother's friend answered. 'I knew it right

away, and so I thought you'd bring him with you. What a good-looking son!'

The children were shouting, the girl was talking, we were in a room with a very high two-poster bed, and my mother said to her friend:

'Go on, throw yourself on the bed!'

'You're going to do it in front of him?' my mother's friend said.

'Why? You want me to send him out?' my mother exclaimed.

'I didn't say that,' my mother's friend replied.

All the children were in the room, even the girl, and the lady friend of my mother's said: 'It makes me a little shy. He's so big!'

My mother laughed and she laughed with my mother. The girl laughed too.

'But I'm the one who made him so big,' my mother said. 'You shouldn't be shy.'

Then my mother's friend threw herself on the bed.

'I imagine he's already seen many women!' she said.

She uncovered herself, and while she waited for my mother to inject her, said:

'I imagine he's seen more appetising women than me.'

The children jumped around, shouting, and my mother, not yet ready to inject her, said, 'Are you afraid of giving him an appetite?'

She laughed, and the girl laughed with her, and while

the children jumped around, my mother's friend laughed against her pillow and exclaimed, 'Oh, no, Concezione! I know perfectly well I could almost be his mother.'

Then I said,' I don't think that matters . . .'

She had a lovely body; I wanted to pay her a compliment. And she cried, 'What are you trying to say?'

And my mother said, 'Are you saying that she gives you an appetite?'

'Why not?' I said.

'Oh!' my mother's friend cried, laughing.

'Oh!' my mother cried, laughing.

The girl laughed with them, the injection was done, and my mother's friend got up to talk to me, laughing, wagging a threatening finger at my chin. 'Do you know what you are?' she said. 'You are impertinent.'

As soon as we were outside my mother asked me:

'Did she really give you an appetite?'

'Why not?' I responded.

'Oh!' my mother exclaimed. And laughed.

'A woman ten years older than you!' she said. And added: 'The widow gave you an appetite, too?'

'Yes!' I answered. 'Even more so . . .'

'Oh!' my mother exclaimed.

She laughed and said, 'If I'd known I wouldn't have let you see.'

But inside she was elated, somehow victorious, as we came to the end of the uphill street and into an open space looking out over the whole valley and the setting sun.

My mother looked at the sun, then asked me:

'When was the first time you saw the shape of a woman's body?'

XXXI

There was still bagpipe music in the great cold air bright with sunlight, and it was alive now, not snow, not cloud, but very close, and in it there was the chiming of the goats' bells, no longer a scattered tinkling but a full chiming, as if herds and herds were passing behind the houses.

'The first time?' I said.

I began to think, trying to remember so I could respond to my mother.

'Yes, the first time you saw the shape of a woman's body,' my mother said.

I tried to remember; I was happy to remember and it was easy enough.

'I think I always knew,' I said.

'Even at ten, when you were just a brat jumping off the train while it was moving?' my mother exclaimed.

'Of course,' I said. 'I knew the shape of a woman's body very well when I was ten.'

'Even at seven?' my mother exclaimed. 'Even at seven, when you were just a tot and sat in my friends' laps?'

'I think so,' I said. 'Even at seven. Where were we living when I was seven?'

My mother counted.

'It was the first year of the war,' she said. 'We were in Terranova. We were in a plate-layer's house less than a mile from town.'

'In Terranova?' I said.

At seven and eight and nine I had read *A Thousand and One Nights* and many other books there, old stories of old journeys, and that was also Sicily for me, *A Thousand and One Nights* and the old countries, trees, houses, and people of far-away times I met through books. Then, in my manhood, I forgot, but I still had it inside me, I could remember, I could rediscover it. Blessed is he who has things to rediscover!

We're lucky to read as children. And doubly lucky to read books about old times and old countries, books of history, books of journeys, and, in a special way, *A Thousand and One Nights*. You can even remember what you've read as if you somehow lived it yourself, and then you have the history of men and all the world inside you, together with your own childhood: Persia when you were seven years old, Australia at eight, Canada at nine, Mexico at ten, and the Hebrews of the Bible with the Tower of Babylon and David, that winter when you were six, caliphs and sultans one February or September, and during the summer the great war with Gustav Adolf et cetera for Sicily-Europe – all in a town like Terranova or Siracusa, while every night the train carries soldiers to a great war which is all wars.

I was lucky enough to read a lot when I was a child, and for me, in Terranova, Sicily was also Baghdad and the Palace of Tears and the Garden of Palms. There I read *A Thousand and One Nights* and other things, in a house which was full of couches and the daughters of some friend of my father's, and from that time I can remember the nakedness of woman, like that of the sultans' wives and the odalisques – a nakedness concrete and certain, the heart and reason of the world.

'Yes, I knew the shape of a woman's body better than ever, when I was seven,' I said.

'Better than ever?' my mother said.

'Better than ever,' I said. 'I knew and I could see it, I always had it right before my eyes, the shape of a woman's body.'

'What are you saying?' my mother exclaimed. 'You thought about it all the time?'

And I: 'No. I didn't think about it. I knew and I saw it before my eyes. That's all. That's enough, isn't it?'

'Who did you see?' my mother asked.

And I: 'Every woman . . . It was very natural for me. There wasn't anything naughty about it.'

That was how it was. There wasn't anything naughty about it. But there was Woman, none the less. At seven, you don't know the world's evils, or sadness, or hopelessness, you aren't agitated by abstract furies, but you know Woman. Never does anyone born male know

Woman the way he does at seven or earlier. Woman is before him, not as a relief, not as a joy, not even as a trick or a game. She is a certainty of the world; immortal.

'Once when I was seven,' I told my mother, 'the daughter of one of our friends got sick and died. She was like the sick people you care for. I don't know if she was proud or humble, but I kept going to her house, I often found myself spending long hours at her bedside. I had known her for a long time; she played with me, took me on her lap, changed her shirt in front of me. While she was sick, every day a woman came to give her an injection, and I was there, I saw her just as I saw the widow and your friend just now. It wasn't the same thing, naturally. There wasn't any question of appetite. But one day she said to me: I'm going to die!'

'And then?' my mother exclaimed.

'Nothing,' I said.

'What do you mean, nothing?' my mother exclaimed. 'She was one of our friends, the Aladinos, she was a beautiful girl . . .'

'It was a house full of beautiful girls, wasn't it?' I said.

'Yes,' my mother recalled. 'Their father came and went from Malta with shiploads of tar and one girl went with him at a time. Then one stayed in Malta, she married a goldsmith. Another married a broker. And this other one died.'

My mother stopped, and asked:

'And so? You were talking about when she died . . .'

'I told you,' I responded. 'She died and I kept going to her house. I looked at her sisters instead of at her.'

'You weren't distressed by her death?' my mother asked.

'I don't know,' I said. 'I saw the others naked like her . . . It was never again as beautiful as that,' I said.

'What?' my mother exclaimed. 'You never saw women shapelier than the Aladino sisters?'

'That's not what I'm saying,' I said.

'And your wife?' my mother exclaimed. 'Isn't your wife at least as good as the Aladino sisters? What kind of wife did you marry?'

'That's not what I'm saying,' I said.

'You haven't seen much in the way of women!' my mother exclaimed.

'That's not what I'm saying,' I said for the third time.

And my mother said:

'Come, now let's go to Miss Elvira's. You'll see how shapely a twenty-year-old girl can be.'

She hastened her step, striding ahead of me through clusters of people and clusters of goats into the great red sun that was setting, and in the midst of the glorious bleating of bagpipe music, she said again:

'Whenever I give an injection to Miss Elvira, I always think, maybe my sons have never seen anything as good as this.'

Part Four

XXXII

But by now I had had enough of those women and sick people, and I annoyed my mother because I wouldn't continue on with her to Miss Elvira's.

We were beneath the building, halfway up the mountain of houses, and I said: 'I'll wait for you here.'

'What nonsense is this?' my mother shouted.

Like an offended mother she turned as if to hit me, but instead of a boy she found a man of thirty, almost a stranger; and instead she shouted. 'What an idiot!' she shouted. But I won, because I really didn't want to go on, the wheel of my journey had stopped in me, for now. What was the good of my seeing another woman? Or even another sick person; what good was it? What good was it for me? What good was it for them?

Death or immortality I was familiar with; and in Sicily or the world it was all the same thing. I looked at the building, and thought of the woman inside ready for my mother's needle, for my eyes, for a man; and I refused to think her any more immortal than any other woman, or than a sick person or a dead person. I sat down on the kerb. 'I'll wait for you here,' I said to my mother again.

Then, while I was waiting, I saw a kite come up over the valley, and I followed it with my eyes as it passed above me into the sunlight high overhead, and I asked myself why, after all, the world was not *A Thousand and One Nights*, the way it was when I was seven. I heard bagpipes, the goats' bells, and voices carrying across the slope of roofs and the valley, and I asked myself this question many times over as I watched the kite in the air. We call them flying dragons in Sicily, as somehow they embody China or Persia in the Sicilian sky, with their sapphire and opal colours and their geometry, and watching it I couldn't help but ask myself why, really, the faith one has at seven doesn't last for ever.

Might it be dangerous, perhaps? At seven, a boy senses miracles in all things, and in their nakedness, in the nakedness of Woman, he has certainty in her as I suppose that she, rib of man, has certainty in us. Death exists, but doesn't take anything away from this certainty; it never wrongs man's world of *A Thousand and One Nights*. A boy asks for nothing but paper and wind, he needs only to launch a kite. He goes outside and launches it; and it is a shout which rises from him, the boy carries it through the spheres with a long, invisible thread, and in this way his faith consummates, celebrates, certainty. But later, what would he do with certainty? Later, one knows the wrongs done to the world, the ruthlessness, the servitude, the injustice among men, and the desecration of earthly life against humanity and against the world. What would one do then, if even still, one had certainty?

What would one do? one asks oneself. What would I do, what would I do? I asked myself.

And the kite passed into the distance, I looked down from the sky and saw a knife grinder who had stopped in front of the building.

XXXIII

Open to the valley, the whole street was in full sunlight, and the sun sparkled on various parts of the knife grinder and his cart. My eyes were dazzled by the light, so that his face looked black.

'Sharpen your knives! Sharpen your knives!' he shouted up to the windows of the building. His voice screeched, stinging glass and stone, and I saw him as a kind of wild bird, with one of those caps on his head that one sees on the heads of scarecrows in the countryside. 'Nothing to sharpen?' he shouted.

He seemed now to turn towards me and I left the kerb, drawing nearer to his voice as I crossed the street.

'I'm talking to you, stranger,' he shouted.

He had big goosefleshed legs and he seemed somehow perched on his trestle, testing his grindstone by spinning it forward and back. 'Don't you have anything to sharpen in this town?' he shouted.

The wheel of my journey began to move in me again,

so I rummaged in my pockets, first in one, then in the other, and while I searched in a third the man continued, 'Don't you have a sword to sharpen? Don't you have a gun?'

I pulled out a penknife, and the man snatched it from my hand and set furiously to sharpening it as he watched me, his face blackened as if from smoke.

I asked him, 'Isn't there much to sharpen in this town?'

'Not much that's worth it,' the knife grinder answered. And he kept watching me, while his fingers danced on the turbine of the grindstone with the little blade between them, and he was laughing, youthful, he was a nice skinny man under his old scarecrow's hat.

'Not much that's worth it,' he said. 'Not much worth the effort. Not much that gives any pleasure.'

'You probably sharpen knives well. You probably sharpen scissors well,' I said.

'Do you think there are still knives and scissors in this world?'

'I thought so. Aren't there any in this town?'

The eyes of the knife grinder sparkled like the flash of knives as he watched me, and from his mouth, wide open in his black face, his voice came out a little rough, with a mocking tone. 'Not in this town, nor in others,' he shouted. 'I pass through a good many towns, and I sharpen things for some fifteen or twenty thousand people, but I never see any knives, never any scissors.'

I said: 'But what do they give you to sharpen, if never any knives or scissors?'

'I always ask the same thing. What are you giving me to sharpen? Don't you have a sword to give me? Don't you have a gun? And I look them in the face, in the eye, and I see how much of what they give me doesn't even deserve to be called a nail.'

He fell silent and also stopped watching me, and bent over his wheel, accelerated his pedal, and ground furiously in concentration for more than a minute. Finally he said: 'I like sharpening a real blade. Throw it and it's a dart, hold it in your fist and it's a dagger. Ah, if everyone still had a real blade!'

I asked, 'Why? Do you think something would happen?'

'Oh, how I'd like to be sharpening a real blade all the time!' the knife grinder answered.

He returned to sharpening in furious concentration for a few seconds, then, relenting, and under his breath, he added: 'Sometimes it seems to me that if everyone had teeth and claws to sharpen, it would be enough. I'd sharpen them like the teeth of vipers, like the claws of a leopard . . .'

He looked at me and winked, his eyes glistening and his face black, and said, 'Ha ha!'

'Ha ha!' I said and winked at him.

He bent towards me and whispered in my ear. And I listened to his words in my ear, laughing 'ha ha!' and I whispered in his ear, and the two of us each whispered in the other's ear, and laughing, slapped the other on the back.

XXXIV

Then the knife grinder gave me my blade, whetted like a dart or a dagger, and when I asked how much it cost, he said forty centimes, and I brought out four pieces of change, ten centimes each, and put them on the shelf of his trestle.

He opened a cash box, and I saw that it was divided in three sections with change of twenty or ten centimes in each one, for a sum total of about five or six lire. I said:

'Slim pickings today!'

But he wasn't listening. He was moving his lips, murmuring, absorbed, turning my change over in his fingers, his murmur little by little getting louder. 'Four for bread,' I heard. 'Four for wine . . .' Then he burst out: 'And the man with the whiskers?'

He began again, more loudly: 'Four for whiskers. Four for bread . . .' Then he burst out: 'And the wine?'

More loudly he began again: 'Four for wine. Four for whiskers . . .' And he burst out, 'And bread?'

Then I said, 'But why don't you put everything together and then divide it?'

'Too risky,' the knife grinder said. 'Sometimes I might eat it all, sometimes I might drink it all . . .' He scratched his neck, and gave me back ten centimes, looking at the sky. 'Keep it,' he said. 'I wanted to get a little more from you but God doesn't want it. It's that little more that's causing all the confusion.'

I put the ten centimes back in my pocket, laughing, and he shifted his gaze from the sky back to earth, satisfied to distribute the three remaining pieces of change among the three sections of his cash box. 'Two for bread, two for wine, and two for whiskers,' he said.

He freed his hands, grasped the shafts of his rickety cart, and went on his way uphill in the fading sunlight.

I didn't hesitate to follow him. 'You're going up that way?' I asked. 'I'll go with you.'

But, satisfied as he was to have resolved the problem, he was no longer cheerful. Instead he was sad and silent. He walked looking into space, wagging his head from left to right and right to left under his old scarecrow's cap. And he was a bit of a scarecrow all over, with his black face, his glittering eyes, his big skinny-man's mouth, his patched jacket, torn trousers, bad shoes, the bony movements of his long legs and knees.

'You must excuse me,' he said suddenly. 'I thought I could get away with it because you're a stranger.'

'Oh, it's nothing,' I said. 'Two pieces of change more or less . . .'

'It's a question of not knowing what rules to follow

with strangers. In other towns there may be knife grinders who charge eighty centimes, and one risks hurting them by asking sixty, don't you think?'

He was a little reanimated, and I was enjoying myself, as we went along another stretch of road in silence. The sun had gone down, and the toll of a bell reached us from the highest perch of the houses.

Then the knife grinder cleared his throat.

'It's a beautiful world.'

And I, too, cleared my throat.

'I suppose so,' I said.

And the knife grinder: 'Light, shadow, cold, hot, joy, joylessness . . .'

And I: 'Hope, charity . . .'

And the knife grinder: 'Childhood, youth, old age . . .'

And I: 'Men, women, children . . .'

And the knife grinder: 'Beautiful women, ugly women, thank God, shrewdness and honesty . . .'

And I: 'Memory, fantasy.'

'What do you mean?' the knife grinder exclaimed.

'Oh, nothing,' I said. 'Bread and wine.'

And the knife grinder: 'Pepperoni, milk, goats, pigs and cows . . . Mice.'

And I: 'Bears, wolves.'

And the knife grinder: 'Birds. Trees and smoke, snow . . .'

And I: 'Sickness, healing. I know, I know. Death, immortality and resurrection.'

'Ah!' the knife grinder shouted.

'What?' I asked.

'It's amazing,' the knife grinder said. 'Ah! and Oh! Uh! Eh!'

And I: 'I suppose so.'

And the knife grinder: 'It's a shame to wrong the world.'

And I didn't say anything more, I found myself once again thinking as I was before I met him, back when the kite was passing through the sky, as if he were now the kite. I looked at him and stopped, and he stopped, too, and asked me: 'Excuse me, if you meet someone you really enjoy meeting, and then take two pieces of change or two lire more from him for a service you should instead give him for free, given the pleasure of knowing him, what are you, a worldly person or one who wrongs the world?'

I started to laugh. 'Oh!' I laughed. And it was genuine.

And he asked: 'Aren't you someone who wrongs the world? Are you worldly? Do you belong to the world?'

'Oh!' I laughed, lightly, since it was genuine.

And he laughed: 'Ha!'

He took off his hat and waved. 'Thanks, friend,' he said. And again he laughed, 'Ha!'

Again I laughed, 'Oh!' And he said: 'Sometimes we confuse the petty things of the world with wrongs to the world.'

Then he began to whisper again in my ear: 'If there were knives and scissors . . .'

And he whispered in my ear, for a minute or two, but

I didn't whisper back; for me, it was as if my kite were whispering.

XXXV

We came to a kind of square very high up, and there was no more sun, no more goats' bells or bagpipes, my mother was gone, the women were gone. The knife grinder pointed out a shop.

'Want to meet someone who has an awl?' he asked me.

A horse's head of painted wood topped the stone arch of the shop and on both sides of the entrance, hanging on the door jambs and on the open doors, I saw ropes and strips of leather with tassels, bells, and multicoloured feathers.

The knife grinder left his rickety cart in the square, and leaped ahead of me onto the threshold, leading me inside. 'Ezechiele!' he shouted. 'Ezechiele!'

Inside there was a long dark hallway, with ropes and strips of leather, tassels, bells and feathers, reins, whips, saddles, and every kind of decoration and harness for horses hanging from the two walls and even suspended from the ceiling.

'Ezechiele!' the knife grinder shouted again as we moved forward.

From behind us someone came running, collided with us with a thud, then went on ahead of us, and a boy's voice burst out:

'It's Calogero, Uncle Ezechiele!'

We kept moving forward through the narrow hallway, through horse decorations and harnesses, saddles, reins, whips, et cetera; we groped our way in perfect darkness, descending into the pure heart of Sicily. The smell was good, in this heart of ours, among the invisible ropes and strips of leather; a smell of new dust, of earth not yet contaminated by the world's wrongs, the wrongs that take place on the earth. Ah, I thought, if I really believed in this . . . And it was not like going underground, it was like following the trajectory of the kite, having the kite before my eyes and nothing else, only darkness, and having a child's heart, Sicilian and all the world's.

Eventually we discerned ahead of us a little light, and the little light became more light and a man took shape, sitting in front of a tiny table with reins and whips and shadows of reins and whips dangling over his head.

'Ezechiele!' the knife grinder called.

The man turned round, and his face looked plump, and his tiny eyes gleamed as if to say: 'Yes, my friend, the world has been wronged, but not yet here, inside!' In a pleasant voice he asked: 'Want the awl, Calogero?'

And then he saw me, and his tiny eyes widened with worry, until the knife grinder, my kite, said: 'I don't need it tonight, Ezechiele. I found a friend who has a blade.'

'Oh, really?' the man exclaimed, and he stood up, short

and plump all over, with curly blond hair and dimples in his cheeks, and his tiny eyes recovered their brightness as if saying again: 'The world has been wronged, but not yet here, inside.'

He looked for something, maybe chairs, under the curtain of leashes and tassles and strips of leather, as he moved there was a sound of bells everywhere, then he sat down again without having found or done a thing.

'Tell him I'm very glad to meet him,' he said to the knife grinder.

Next to the table there was a wooden ladder hidden among the harnesses hanging from the ceiling, and the knife grinder leaned on it with one hand. 'He's very glad to meet you, too,' he answered.

'Very much so,' I said.

And the man examined me, smiling, sure in himself that I was glad to meet him because the knife grinder had said so, not because I said so. It was with the knife grinder that he continued to speak. 'It seems clear enough to me,' he said, still examining me.

'I saw it right away,' the knife grinder answered. 'There's no mistaking it.'

And the man Ezechiele: 'No, there's no mistaking it.'

And the knife grinder: 'He's suffering.'

And the man Ezechiele: 'Yes, he's suffering.'

And the knife grinder: 'He's suffering the pain of the wronged world. He's not suffering for himself.'

And the man Ezechiele: 'Not for himself, that's understood. Everyone suffers for himself, yet . . .'

And the knife grinder: 'Yet there're no knives and no scissors, there's never anything . . .'

And the man Ezechiele: 'Nothing. No one knows anything, no one notices anything . . .'

They fell silent, and looked at one another, and the eyes of the man Ezechiele filled with sadness, while the eyes of the knife grinder glistened more whitely than ever, as if almost frightened, in his black face.

'Oh!' the knife grinder said.

'Oh!' the man Ezechiele said.

And they moved closer together, and leaning over the little table, each whispered in the other's ear. Then the knife grinder, turning round, said: 'But our friend has a little blade. And he's suffering the pain of the wronged world.'

'Yes,' the man Ezechiele said. And he looked at me, his tiny eyes glistening sadly as if to say: 'The world has been badly wronged, very very badly, more than we ourselves know.'

Then he turned again to look at the knife grinder.

'Did you tell him how we're suffering?' he asked.

'I began to tell him,' the knife grinder responded.

And the man Ezechiele: 'Good, tell him we're not suffering for ourselves.'

'That he knows,' the knife grinder responded.

And the man Ezechiele: 'Tell him that there's nothing making us suffer for ourselves, we're not burdened with sickness, we're not hungry, and still we suffer a lot, oh, a lot!'

And the knife grinder: 'He knows, he knows!'

And the man Ezechiele: 'Ask him if he really knows.'

And the knife grinder to me, 'Truly, you know, don't you?'

I nodded my head. And the man Ezechiele stood up, clapped his hands, and called: 'Achille!'

From the thick of the harnesses appeared the boy who had collided with us in the hallway. 'Why don't you stay here and listen?' the man Ezechiele asked him.

The boy was very small, with blond curly hair like his uncle's. 'I was listening, Uncle Ezechiele,' he responded.

The man Ezechiele approved and again turned to the knife grinder.

'So,' he said, 'our friend knows that we're suffering the pain of the wronged world.'

'He knows,' the knife grinder said.

The man Ezechiele began to recapitulate: 'The world is big and it is beautiful, but it has been badly wronged. Everyone suffers each for himself, but not for the world that has been wronged and so it continues to be wronged.'

He looked around him as he spoke, and his tiny eyes closed in sadness, then opened and looked eagerly for the knife grinder: 'And did you tell our friend,' he said, 'that I am writing down the pains of the wronged world?'

In fact he had a kind of notebook on his tiny table, and an inkpot, a pen.

'Did you tell him, Calogero?' he said.

The knife grinder answered: 'I was about to tell him.'

And he said: 'Good, you can tell our friend. Tell him that like an ancient hermit I spend my days here writing the history of the wronged world. Tell him that I'm suffering but I write, and that I'm writing down all the wrongs one by one, and I'm also writing about all the evildoers who laugh over the wrongs they have done and will do.'

'Knives, scissors, pikes,' the knife grinder shouted.

And the man Ezechiele placed a hand on the head of the boy and pointed to me, 'Do you see this friend of ours?' he said. 'Like your uncle, he's suffering. He's suffering the pain of the wronged world. Learn, Achille. And now, watch the shop while we go for a glass of wine at Colombo's.'

XXXVI

So we went out into the open and it was dusk. The bells of the Ave Maria were ringing.

The knife grinder grasped the shafts of his rolling cart and began to push it, walking, and I walked with him, and the man Ezechiele walked between us, a little man taking little steps, wrapped in a shawl.

'The world is terribly wronged! The world is terribly

wronged!' his eyes said, looking around with sadness. Then they rested on the knife grinder's cart as it rolled along.

'What do you have there, Calogero, on your grindstone?' he asked, stopping.

'What?' the knife grinder asked, stopping also.

'It's a slip of paper,' I said.

And the knife grinder let out a shout. 'Damn it,' he shouted. 'Again!'

'A fine again?' the man Ezechiele asked.

And the knife grinder shouted, 'Again!'

He raised his arms to the sky, made two or three odd jumps in the air, bit his hands, and took off his scarecrow's hat and flung it to the ground.

'But this is how . . . this is how . . .' he was saying. 'It's the third time in a month!' he shouted. 'Scissors, awls, knives and pikes; mortars, scythes, and hammers, guns, guns, dynamite and a hundred thousand volts . . .'

Ezechiele now made the gesture of Joshua when he stopped the sun.

And the knife grinder stopped.

'My friend,' the man Ezechiele said.

'Yes, my friend,' the knife grinder answered.

'What do we suffer for?' the man Ezechiele asked.

'What?' the knife grinder answered. 'The pain of wronged humanity.'

And the man Ezechiele: 'And therefore not for ourselves. For the pain of the wronged world. Not for ourselves . . .'

And the knife grinder: 'Not for ourselves, that goes without saying.'

And he fell silent, grasped his cart again by the shafts, went back to pushing it, and with him we all moved again.

'But how will I pay?' he grumbled.

He seemed to hear something worrisome and again he stopped, and shook his cart while he stood and listened.

'I don't hear the money,' he said.

It was almost dark, late dusk, and his eyes gleamed like the sharpened white blades of knives in the black of his face. And he opened the little cash drawer, looked inside, opened it even more, pulled it all the way out, turned it over. Nothing fell out, and the man Ezechiele said:

'Remember, we're not suffering for ourselves.'

'I remember,' the knife grinder grumbled.

And the man Ezechiele asked:

'How much was there?'

The knife grinder answered: 'There was enough for bread, there was enough for wine, and there was enough for taxes, two-thirty, two-thirty, and two-thirty, a fairly good day.'

'Good,' the man Ezechiele said, 'the wine you'll have with me now, at Colombo's, and the bread I can offer you tonight at my table, if you'll let me . . .'

'Yes,' the knife grinder continued, 'and I'll cover my head with the revered hat of my grandfather, I'll protect my shoulders with the blessed jacket of my father, I'll hide my privates in the trousers of the priest Orazio, and my feet . . . There's a lot of goodness among men, a lot of goodness, and I can take shelter in a warm home with Gonzales's cows. Why work at even one of my three trades? Only to live by charity, as the Nazarene prescribed . . .'

'But, son,' the man Ezechiele said, 'your money might have been taken by a poor vagrant . . . He might have been without food or drink for a long time. You can only be glad to have given him the means to slake his hunger and thirst.'

The knife grinder kept silent and began again to push his rickety cart, and as he walked he sighed. Then, as he walked, he spoke.

'Right!' he said. 'Right! These aren't the world's wrongs we can suffer for. These are only petty things between the poor men of the world. Oh, knives! Oh, scissors! There's so much more in the world that wrongs the world!'

'So much more!' the man Ezechiele murmured.

'So much more! So much more!' the knife grinder shouted. 'And the petty things are only petty, little pranks between man and man inside the circle of the world! Who has never played a little prank on his fellow man, thrown the first stone . . . ? I myself played one on our friend today!'

'Oh, yes?' the man Ezechiele exclaimed, and laughed.

'Yes, a little prank of two pieces of change,' the knife grinder said, and he, too, laughed.

I laughed also, and the little prank was recounted, and we laughed all three together like childhood friends. 'Still, this vagrant could have left me the money for the taxes,' the knife grinder said.

He stopped laughing and his eyes shone like the white blades of explosive knives.

'Oh, awls!' he shouted. 'And what if this vagrant was the same dogcatcher who gave me the fine? It isn't the first time my day's earnings vanish just when the fine appears.'

The man Ezechiele grasped him and held him tightly in his arms. 'Coincidence!' he said. 'These are not the kind of wrongs for which we suffer.'

XXXVII

The cold air was clear, calm, and the bells, no longer flying against the sky, were quiet in their nests. But one could still distinguish colours in the little street, and I cried:

'Look! A flag!'

'Flag?' the knife grinder said.

And the man Ezechiele: 'What flag?'

'On that door,' I said.

And the man Ezechiele: 'That's Porfirio! He's the cloth merchant!'

My two companions laughed, and I remembered that in Sicily it was the tradition to indicate a fabric shop by hanging a strip of cloth outside the door. It didn't matter what colour the cloth was; it could be green, yellow, blue; but a strip of cloth meant that a cloth merchant was selling fabrics there. In this case the strip of cloth was red, and the knife grinder said, turning to me: 'Porfirio has half a pair of scissors.'

'Oh, yes?' I said.

'Yes,' the knife grinder said, 'and sometimes, when I don't want to be bothering Ezechiele for the awl all the time, I make Porfirio give me his scissors.'

Ezechiele proposed: 'Maybe this is the chance to introduce our friend to Porfirio.'

'Maybe so,' the knife grinder said.

They took me inside and the knife-grinding contraption stayed on the street once again. But the shop was not deep, it was a kind of alcove with the fabrics heaped up in tall stacks on a few chairs all close to the door.

'Come in, please,' a clear voice invited us into the dark interior.

'Good evening,' they greeted each other. 'Good evening.'

And the voice continued, 'Good evening. I was just about to close up.'

'And you leave the strip of cloth outside?' the knife grinder asked.

'No, I was just about to bring it in,' the voice answered.

And the man Ezechiele said: 'Red again, today.'

And the voice: 'Yes, I've been putting red up for quite a while. But tomorrow I'm changing it to dark blue.'

And the man Ezechiele: 'Yes! The world is full of variety!'

And the voice: 'Various! Beautiful! Large!'

'And very wronged, very wronged!' murmured the man Ezechiele.

The knife grinder said then: 'Tell him about our friend, Ezechiele.'

'What friend?' the voice asked.

A human form moved, behind the voice, in the dark, and it seemed as if all the dark was moving: he was gigantic. Distinct from this bulk of man, coming close to me in the light from the door, the lovely warm voice asked again: 'What friend? This gentleman here?'

'This gentleman,' the man Ezechiele responded. 'Like you, Porfirio, and like Calogero the knife grinder, like me, and no doubt like many others on the face of the earth, he is someone who suffers the pain of the wronged world.'

'Ah!' exclaimed the immense man.

He came even closer to me and a warm breeze, his breath, ruffled the hairs on my forehead. 'Ah!' he exclaimed again.

His large hand descended from above, searched for mine and clasped it in a grip which, despite all, was kind. 'I'm delighted,' he said above my head. And turning back to the others he said:

'He suffers, you said?'

His breath was a warm sirocco in my hair and, still holding my hand with a kindly strength, the man repeated: 'I'm delighted.'

'Thank you,' I said. 'It's nothing.'

'Oh!' the man said. 'It's a lot. I'm very honoured.'

And I: 'The honour is mine.'

And the man: 'No, all mine, sir.' And again turning back to the others, while my hair flew under his breath, again he asked: 'So he's suffering?'

'Yes, Porfirio,' the man Ezechiele responded. 'He's suffering, and not for himself.'

'Not for the little things of the world,' the knife grinder explained. 'Not because they gave him a fine, not because he tried to play a little prank on his fellow man . . .'

'No,' the man Ezechiele said. 'It's a universal pain that he's suffering.'

And the knife grinder said: 'The pain of the wronged world.'

In the dark the enormous man Porfirio touched my head, my face, and again exclaimed: 'Ah!' Then he said: 'I understand and I appreciate it.'

'Scissors and knives!' the knife grinder shouted.

'Scissors?' the man Porfirio repeated softly. He was a mass of darkness, with a heat which came from some part of him to flow among us like a beneficent current of the gulf, with a wind above, and with a sweet, deep voice. 'Knives?' he repeated. And sweetly, deeply he said:

'No, friends, not knives, not scissors, none of all that is necessary, only the living water . . .'

'Living water?' murmured the knife grinder.

'Living water?' murmured the man Ezechiele, too.

And the man Porfirio continued: 'I've told you a thousand times and I'll tell you again. Only the living water can wash away the wrongs of the world and slake the thirst of wronged humanity. But where is the living water?'

'Where there are knives there is living water,' the knife grinder said.

'Where there is suffering for the world there is living water,' said the man Ezechiele.

We were immersed in night now, and our voices were lowered, no one could have heard us talking any more. We were close together, with our heads close together, and the man Porfirio was like an enormous black Saint Bernard who held himself and everyone else gathered up in the heat of his fur. For a long time he talked of the living water; and the man Ezechiele talked, the knife grinder talked; and the words were night in the night and we were shadows. I thought I had joined a furtive gathering of spirits. Then the voice of the man Porfirio rose. 'Let's go. I'm offering you a glass of wine at Colombo's,' he said. And he pulled down the cloth hanging over the door, closed the door, and led us, wrapped in his warm current, along the street.

XXXVIII

Only inside Colombo's did he take on colour and shape. He appeared to be over six feet tall and three feet wide, dressed in brown fur, with a full head of salt and pepper hair, blue eyes, a chestnut beard, and red hands: with his generous gaze, truly a big Saint Bernard.

'Hello, Colombo!' he said as he entered.

Even the little knife-grinding contraption came in with us, and the pub was lit with kerosene burners, and men were singing: '*And the blood of Santa Bumbila.*'

Colombo, behind the bar, had a yellow handkerchief like a pirate's round his head.

'*Olé,*' he answered.

And the man Ezechiele said: 'Wine. These men are my guests.'

'Yours?' the man Porfirio gently protested. 'I invited everyone.'

The men who were singing were sitting on a bench against the wall, without a table in front of them, and they held little iron mugs in their hands, swaying their heads and bodies simultaneously as they sang.

'But I invited them first,' Ezechiele explained.

'Your wine,' Colombo said, and set four full mugs on the bar. Then he added, smiling: 'This can be Mr Ezechiele's round. And then there can be Mr Porfirio's round.'

'Of course,' said the man Ezechiele.

'I understand and I appreciate it,' said the man Porfirio. And he raised his mug: 'I'm very honoured.'

The man Ezechiele bowed. I bowed too. And the knife grinder shouted: '*Viva!*'

There was a brazier lit in the middle of this pub without tables, and two young ploughmen crouched near it were warming their hands. Colombo poured out wine from a cask, prepared new mugs, and the men on the bench swayed, singing softly, and from the ground, from the walls, from the darkness, came the age-old odour of wine accumulated upon wine. The whole past of wine in human life was present around us.

'*Viva* what?' asked the man Ezechiele.

'*Viva* this!' the knife grinder answered, raising his mug.

'This?' said the man Porfirio. 'What's this?'

He drank and everyone drank, I drank, too, and the tankards resounded emptily on the wet zinc of the bar. Colombo returned from the cask with more wine.

'The world,' the knife grinder shouted. 'Earth, wood, and dwarves in the forest; a beautiful woman, night and morning, sun, light; smoke for honeying, love, joy and weariness; and sleep without wrongs, the world without wrongs . . .'

'*And the blood of Santa Bumbila,*' the men on the bench sang hoarsely.

We were on the second tankard, the nonsense lyric

fell on deaf air and deaf walls. 'I don't think so,' said the man Porfirio.

'All the same,' the man Ezechiele said.

'No, we need the living water,' said the man Porfirio.

'*Olé*, living water!' shouted Colombo the barkeeper. 'Here's the living water! Isn't this living water? Listen, men: joy, life, living water . . .'

The man Porfirio shook his enormous head but he drank, and everyone drank, I drank too, and the two ploughmen near the brazier drank with their greedy eyes, and the men on the bench sang into their drained mugs. 'Trees and fresh figs, pine needles,' the knife grinder continued, 'stars in honoured hearts, incense and myrrh, mermaids of the deep sea, free legs, free arms, free chests, hair and skin in the wind in freedom, a free race, a free fight, uh! oh! ah!'

'Ah aaah! Ah aaah! Ah aaah?' sang the men on the bench. 'Ah! Ah!' said the two sitting close to the brazier. Other men came in. Colombo shouted *olé* and poured out wine, and he, too, was drinking, and under the dark vault there was nothing but wine naked across the centuries and men naked in the whole past of wine, the musty nude smell of wine, the nudity of wine.

'Drink, friend!' the knife grinder said to me, and he handed me the third mug.

The man Porfirio noted: 'Our friend is an out-of-towner.'

'Yes, he's an out-of-towner,' the man Ezechiele confirmed. 'He met Calogero first.'

'He has a blade,' the knife grinder cried. 'He has the living water. He suffers for the wronged world, and the world is large, the world is beautiful, the world is a bird and has milk, gold, fire, thunder and floods. Living water to him who has the living water!'

'Here's the living water, men,' said Colombo. And he, too, drank, he, too, was naked in the nudity of wine, he was the dwarf in the mine of wine.

'I'm not that much of an out-of-towner,' I answered the man Porfirio.

'Not that much?' said the man Ezechiele.

'What do you mean, not that much?' asked the man Porfirio.

Drinking slowly from my third mug I explained that I wasn't so much of an out-of-towner, and the tiny eyes of the man Ezechiele gleamed with satisfaction.

'Ah! But look!' exclaimed the man Porfirio.

'Didn't you know that he's one of Ferrauto's sons?' said the dwarf Colombo.

And the knife grinder shouted: 'Ferrauto has many knives. *Viva* Ferrauto!' Everyone was at the bottom of the third mug, but I was still only halfway through mine, and the knife grinder threw the rest on the ground, he said I must have a fourth with them.

'I knew your grandfather,' the man Porfirio said.

'Who didn't know him?' the knife grinder cried. 'He had the living water.'

'Yes,' said the man Porfirio. 'He came here with me, we drank together . . .'

'He was a great drinker,' observed Colombo the dwarf.

From the bench against the wall the men sang now with melancholy. '*And the blood of Santa Bumbila,*' they still sang, and swayed their heads, their torsos; they were mournfully naked in the original nudity of wine.

'He, too, suffered for the wronged world,' the man Ezechiele said.

'The wronged world? What wronged world?' cried the wanton dwarf of wine.

'And I knew your father, too,' said the man Porfirio.

'We were friends,' added the man Ezechiele. 'He was a poet and Shakespearean actor. Macbeth, Hamlet, Brutus . . . Once he gave us a reading.'

'Oh, a magnificent event,' the knife grinder cried. 'Knives and tridents! Red-hot irons!'

Everyone drank from the fourth mug, I was the only one holding mine still untouched, listening to them talk about my father in the presence of wine.

'We came here to drink together,' said the man Porfirio.

And the wanton gnome observed: 'It was here he gave that reading. He came with a red cape and told me I was the king of Denmark.'

'He told me I was Polonius,' the man Ezechiele murmured humbly. Then he added, 'Oh, he suffered much for the wronged world!'

Here the knife grinder cried again: '*Viva!*'

And the man Porfirio asked again: '*Viva* what?'

'*Viva! Viva!*' the knife grinder cried.

'*Viva!*' cried a drunk.

'*Viva!*' cried another drunk.

'*Viva!*' the man Ezechiele murmured humbly.

'And *viva, viva, viva!*' sang the melancholy men swaying on the bench.

Thus those who suffered personal misfortune and those who suffered the pain of the wronged world were together in the nude tomb of wine, and could be like spirits, finally parted from this world of suffering and wrongs.

Seated on the ground near the brazier, the two young men without wine were crying.

XXXIX

'Another round for me and my friends,' the man Porfirio ordered.

He had unbuttoned the enormous pelt in which he lived, revealing his limbs; and the man Ezechiele had freed himself from the entanglement of his shawl. 'It'll be the last round,' the man Porfirio said, 'but just one more round.'

He had already drunk six mugs. Ezechiele and the knife grinder had drunk five. I was still on my fourth, which was almost full. With his red hands and face, his white and chestnut beard, and his white and black hair, Porfirio, enormous, towered over that underground of wine. He was a man, he didn't belong to the wine like Colombo the gnome, but he was a great conquering king who lived in this, his conquered underworld, in wine.

Yet he denied that wine was living water and he did not forget the world. 'Don't fool yourselves, don't fool yourselves,' he said.

'What?' said the knife grinder.

And the man Ezechiele looked around with his tiny eyes in sudden consternation. 'No!' his eyes seemed to shout. And then the man Porfirio, wrapping his red hand round the handle of his seventh mug, assured him that where there was wine there was none of the world's pettiness.

'But the wrongs of the world? The terrible wrongs to humanity and to the world?' asked the man Ezechiele.

I (I repeat) was still on my fourth mug. Something had stopped me at the beginning of it and I couldn't drink any more, I didn't dare advance any further into the squalid nudity, the groundless territory of wine.

'Drink, friend,' the man Porfirio encouraged me.

I tried and took a sip between my lips and the wine seemed good, by itself, just that sip between my lips, but even so I couldn't drink it; all the human past in me told me it was not something living, pressed from the summer and the earth, but a sad, sad thing, a phantom pressed from the caverns of centuries. And what else could it be in a world always wronged? Generation after generation had drunk, had poured out its pain in wine, sought nudity in wine, and one generation drank from another, from the nudity of the squalid wine of past generations, and from all the pain that had been poured out.

'*And the blood of Santa Bumbila*,' sang the melancholy men on the bench.

By now everyone in the pub was hanging his head low, everyone was melancholy. The knife grinder was melancholy with an explosive look in his eye. Ezechiele was melancholy with a frightened look in his eye; he looked around in anxious panic, seeing once again the shapes of the wronged world.

He had been Polonius for my Shakespearean father. And the man Porfirio? What could the man Porfirio have been for my father Hamlet? He was the only one who was serene, because he was the only one without illusions, and yet he was gravely responsible. He looked at us: me, Ezechiele, the knife grinder, the drunks on their feet in front of the bar, the two young men crying as they sat on the ground in front of the brazier, and the men on the bench singing. Melancholy, the men on the bench swayed their heads as they sang, and it seemed that they swayed them the way some do when crying, and their song was a hoarse lamentation. For a long time the man Porfirio looked at them, and then he looked at Ezechiele, me, and the knife grinder once more; he looked at the two young men crying who had not drunk anything the whole night; and I thought maybe he was dismayed to have dragged us along with him, so many men, into that squalor of conquered underground. But instead he was serene, and withdrew into a mystical rapport with the gnome Colombo.

He no longer looked at anyone; he was laughing and he didn't see anything before him but naked happiness provided by the gnome of wine, by Colombo. And he existed at the origins of wine, and was naked in blessed sleep even while standing; he was the ancient, laughing sleeper who sleeps across the centuries of man, the Father Noah of wine.

I recognised him and put my mug down, this was not what I wanted to believe in, there was no world in this, and I left, crossed the little street, and went to where my mother lived.

XL

The house was on the edge of the slope towards the valley. I climbed the outside staircase, I was on the landing. I knew that instead of going in, instead of looking for food or going to bed, I would rather be on the train, and I stopped.

The cold was intense, and below me there were lights; above me, too, in scattered little groups of four or five. The air was blue. The ice of a large desolate star glittered in the sky.

It was night over Sicily and the quiet earth: the wronged world was covered with darkness, men were shut in their rooms with lights lit beside them, and the dead, all those who had been killed, had awakened to sit in their tombs, meditating. I stood thinking, and the great night was in me, night on top of night. Those lights below, above, and that cold in the darkness, that ice of a star in the sky – they didn't belong to one night alone, they were infinite; and I thought of the nights of my grandfather, the nights of my father, and the nights of Noah, the nights of a man naked in wine and defenceless, humiliated, less of a man than a little boy, or one of the dead.

Part Five

XLI

It came to me then that in Sicily the name of the road nearby, *Belle Signore*, Lovely Ladies, was associated with the night: it referred to the Spirits.

A man, still naked and defenceless, would go out into the night and encounter the Spirits, the Lovely Bad Ladies who would tease and mock him, and even trample him, all Phantoms of human action, the wrongs against the world and against humanity risen out of the past. They weren't really the dead but phantoms; they didn't belong to the earthly world. And the man rendered defenceless by wine or by something else was generally their prey.

The man would talk of kings and heroes. And he would let them lay hold of the remains of his conscience, he would accept ancient wrongs to attain glory.

But some, like Shakespeare or my Shakespearean father, would instead take hold of these phantoms and enter them, would wake in their mud and dreams, make them confess their guilt, suffer for man, cry for man, speak for man, become symbols of human liberation. Some, like my father, in wine, some not. One great

Shakespeare, in the purity of his nights of fearless medi-
tation, and my little father in the foolish obscurity of his
nights grown larger in wine.

This was the terrible thing for my father, that he was
naked and foolish in his wine, the poor man. A Noah
covering himself with a pitiful cloth, not a man of signs
and portents.

But I didn't know it at the time.

We would wait a long time by the window for night to
arrive, and it would fill the round flat countryside, barren
of trees, barren of leaves. My father would emerge already
dressed for the reading and his men would emerge too.

'Ready?' he would say. And he would take the horn he
used as head of the railway gang down from the wall.

Noiselessly we would get on the handtruck, we who
were Hamlet's. My mother would take her place in the
middle, with a chair. We gathered round her feet, and
my father manoeuvred from the front while two men
pushed. This was how the handtruck was used: for the
shovel work along the tracks by day, for Hamlet at night.
The two men would push for a moment, then, as we
began to go down a hill, they would jump on too, and
no one would talk any more, the handtruck would roll
by itself, towards the waiting room in a railway station
if it was winter, or, if it was summer, towards a railway
platform where the recital would take place in the open,
in front of the harvesters come from the wheat, among
shouts and bonfires, with my father, possessed, standing
on a stage of railway sleepers.

Oh, the night, back then!

From the ends of the earth dogs barked at the horizons; and the seven invisible heavens, the mountains of Via Lattea, were full of jasmine. Ten, fifteen stars came out; we could smell the fragrance of millions more. And my father blew the horn to begin.

First he heard something, and shouted:

'Who goes there?'

He was referring to some other handcart on the line, ahead of us.

'Polonius' was the response.

Or else:

'Fortinbras.'

Or else:

'Horatio.'

And all of them were naked and foolish men who, by virtue of wine, were taking hold of phantoms.

'Oh, wronged world! Wronged world!' I cried at the thought. I didn't expect any response, unless from memory, but one came up from the ground below. It was a voice that said: 'Ahem!'

XLII

'Some other knife grinder,' I thought.

I looked below, searching, and saw nothing but the

usual lights in the quiet cold.

'Who is it?' I called.

'Ahem!' the voice responded again.

I looked, searching more carefully, and then I saw that the lights were not the usual lights of the closed-up rooms where the men lived. Those had been turned out, it seemed. The new ones burned a pale red in the open night, like railway lanterns placed on the ground in the valley. But I was looking for whoever had said, 'Ahem!'

'Ahem?' I said. 'Ahem?'

'Ahem! Ahem! Ahem!' the terrible voice responded.

I decided to go down to look for it and descended, and when I found myself among those lights which seemed like abandoned lanterns, I discovered that they were the lights of the dead. 'Oh, I'm in the cemetery,' I said.

'Ahem!' the voice responded.

'Who are you?' I asked. 'Are you the gravedigger?'

The voice answered: 'No, no. I'm a soldier.'

I tried to force myself to see in the darkness. The voice sounded nearby, but the lights of the dead gave no illumination around them. 'Strange!' I said.

The soldier laughed: 'Strange?'

'Are you on guard here, maybe?' I asked him.

'No,' said the soldier. 'I'm resting.'

'Here among the tombs?' I exclaimed.

'They are nice comfortable tombs,' the soldier said.

And I said: 'Maybe you came to think about your

loved ones who have died.'

'No,' the soldier answered. 'At most, I think about my loved ones who are living.'

'Ah!' I said. 'About your lady love, I imagine.'

And the soldier: 'A little about everyone. About my mother and my brothers, and my friends, and the friends of my friends, and about my father in *Macbeth*.'

'Your father in *Macbeth*?' I exclaimed.

'Certainly, sir,' the soldier responded. 'He used to recite the part of the king, poor man.'

'How can that be?' I exclaimed.

'Oh, yes!' the soldier said. 'They think that the gods tolerate in kings that which they abhor in common people.'

'But how can that be?' I exclaimed once more. 'My father is like that, too . . .'

'Well,' the soldier observed, 'all fathers are like that. And my brother Silvestro . . .'

I burst out with a kind of shout: 'Your brother Silvestro?'

'Why are you shouting?' the soldier asked. 'There's nothing unusual about having a brother Silvestro, poor boy.'

'No,' I said. 'But Silvestro is my name.'

'So what?' the soldier said. 'There are many more people than there are names.'

I asked: 'Is your brother thirty years old?'

'No, sir,' the soldier answered. 'He's a little boy of eleven or twelve, wearing short socks, with a head thick with hair, and he's in love. He loves, loves the world. He's like me now . . .'

'Like you?' I murmured.

'Yes,' the soldier answered. 'Nothing could wrong us in our love, him as a little boy, and me . . .'

'You as what?' I murmured.

The soldier laughed. 'Ahem!' he laughed.

I reached out a hand. 'Where are you?'

'Here,' the soldier said.

I moved towards the voice, searching with my hand, but found nothing. The lightless lamps of the dead already formed a long road behind me and there were still many around me, in front of me. 'Where are you?' I asked once again.

'Here, here,' the soldier said.

'Ah, over here?' I exclaimed.

'Yes,' he responded. 'Over here.'

'How do you mean?' I exclaimed. 'To the left, then!'

'Ahem!' the soldier said.

I stopped. I was probably at the bottom of the valley: now the lamps of the dead also shone higher above me, without illuminating anything. 'So,' I cried. 'Are you there or aren't you?'

The soldier answered: 'That's what I ask myself, sometimes. Am I here, or aren't I? Anyway, I'm able to remember. And see . . .'

'What else?' I asked.

'That's plenty,' the soldier said. 'I see my brother and I want to play with him.'

'Oh!' I exclaimed. 'You want to play with a little boy of eleven?'

'Why not?' the soldier answered. 'He's bigger than me. If he's eleven, I'm seven.'

I cried: 'How can you be a seven-year-old soldier?'

The soldier sighed and in a tone of reproof said: 'I imagine I suffered enough to attain that.'

'That?' I said. 'To be a soldier?'

'No,' he said. 'To be seven. To play with my brother.'

'Are you playing with your brother now?' I asked him.

'Yes, sir,' he answered. 'By your leave, I am playing, too.'

'Too?' I noted. 'What else are you doing?'

'I'm doing a lot of other things,' he answered. 'I'm talking with a girl. I'm pruning a vine. I'm watering a garden. I'm running . . .'

'Oh, you're forgetting that you're among these tombs,' I said.

'Not at all,' he answered. 'I know perfectly well that I'm here, too, and that nothing can hurt me . . . I'm at peace, as far as that goes.'

'So you're happy,' I observed.

He sighed again. 'How can I be? I've been lying on a field covered with snow and blood for thirty days.'

'But what nonsense are you talking now?' I exclaimed.

This time the soldier didn't respond right away; and for a moment I could hear the great silence that stood between us. 'Ahem!' the soldier said.

'Ahem!' I said.

And the soldier: 'You're right. Excuse me. It was my manner of speaking.'

I took a deep breath, satisfied, and once again instinctively reached out my hand. 'Where are you?'

'Here,' the soldier said.

XLIII

I searched for a few minutes as I had done the first time, to the left and to the right, then I gave up. 'It's too dark,' I said.

'Indeed,' he answered.

And I sat down on a tomb with the lamp of the dead one beside me.

'It's better to sit down.'

'Better this way,' the soldier answered. 'Especially since we're about to have the play.'

'The play?' I exclaimed. 'What play?'

'Didn't you come for the play?' the soldier said.

And I: 'I don't know anything about plays.'

And the soldier: 'Oh, sit and you'll see . . . Here they are, they're arriving now.'

And I: 'Who's arriving?'

The soldier: 'All of them, kings and their opponents, victors and vanquished . . .'

I: 'Really? I don't see anyone . . .'

The soldier: 'That may be because of the dark.'

I: 'So why are they doing a play?'

The soldier: 'They have to. They belong to history . . .'

I: 'And what are they putting on?'

The soldier: 'The acts for which they have been glorified.'

I: 'What? Every night?'

The soldier: 'Eternally, sir. Until Shakespeare puts it all in verse, and avenges the vanquished and gives pardon to the victors.'

I: 'What?'

The soldier: 'You heard me.'

And I: 'But that's terrible.'

The soldier: 'It's frightening.'

I: 'I imagine that they suffer a great deal. The unwritten Caesars. The unwritten Macbeths.'

The soldier: 'And their followers, the partisans, the soldiers . . . We do suffer, sir.'

I: 'You too?'

The soldier: 'Me too.'

I: 'But why you?'

The soldier: 'I'm in the play, too.'

And I: 'You're in the play? You're in the play now?'

The soldier: 'For ever. Since thirty days ago.'

I: 'But didn't you say you were playing with your eleven-year-old brother?'

The soldier: 'Yes. And I'm talking with a girl, I'm pruning a vine, I'm watering a garden . . .'

I: 'Well, then?'

180

The soldier didn't respond.

'Well, then?' I insisted.

The soldier responded: 'Ahem!'

'Ahem? Why ahem?' I cried.

Again the soldier didn't respond.

'Hello?' I called.

'Hello,' the soldier responded.

I: 'I was afraid you had left.'

He: 'No, I'm here.'

I: 'I don't want you to leave.'

He: 'I'm not leaving.'

'Good,' I said.

I hesitated. I said, 'Good,' again. Again I hesitated. Again I said, 'Good.' Finally I asked: 'Is it hard?'

'Alas, yes,' he answered. 'Tied up like a slave, wounded more each day on that field of snow and blood.'

'Oh!' I cried. 'That's the play you're putting on?'

'Exactly,' the soldier responded. 'Of this glory, I am part.'

I said: 'And is it a lot to suffer?'

'A lot,' he said. 'Millions of times over.'

I: 'Millions of times?'

He: 'For every printed word, every pronouncement, every millimetre of bronze erected.'

I: 'It makes you weep?'

He: 'It makes us weep.'

'But still,' I said, 'you're playing with your brother and talking with that girl, you're doing all those other things . . . Isn't that a consolation?'

'I don't know,' the soldier responded.

'Isn't it enough?' I asked.

'I don't know,' the soldier responded again.

I said: 'You're hiding something from me. It seemed you were at peace and that nothing could hurt you . . .'

'That's true,' the soldier responded.

'Then,' I cried, 'it's not true that you weep.'

'Alas!' the soldier sighed.

In a humble voice I asked him, 'Isn't there anything I can do to console you?'

Again he said he didn't know.

And I suggested: 'Maybe a cigarette.'

I looked in my pockets for my cigarettes, and added: 'Do you want to try?'

'Let's try,' he answered.

I held out the cigarette. 'Here,' I said.

But the cigarette remained in my hand. 'Where are you?' I called.

'I'm here,' the soldier said.

I got up, took a step forward, another step, and kept holding out the cigarette, but the cigarette stayed in my hand.

'Well, do you want it or not?' I cried.

'I want it, I want it,' the soldier answered.

I cried out: 'Take it, then.'

The soldier didn't answer.

'Take it. Where are you?' I cried.

Again the soldier didn't answer. And I continued to cry out; I began to run, and I found myself out of the valley, once again on the landing of my mother's house; I could see the cemetery far away below me, with its lights.

XLIV

I slept the rest of that night, and forgot everything, but when I awoke it was still night.

Cold ashes wrapped Sicily and in the icy mountains the sun had not come up, it was as if it would never come up again. It was night without the calm of night, without sleep; ravens flew through the air; and every once in a while, from the roofs or from the gardens, there was a shot.

'What day is it?' I asked my mother.

'Wednesday,' my mother answered.

She was at peace, once again wearing her shawl round her shoulders, and the big men's shoes on her feet, but in a withdrawn mood, not wanting to talk.

'I'm leaving today,' I told her.

My mother shrugged, sitting there with the ash that was wrapped round Sicily sprinkled on her head.

'But what is that noise?' I cried.

I got up and went out onto the landing, and my mother slowly followed me, as if she were keeping an eye on me.

Bang! went a gun.

'What are they shooting at?' I asked.

My mother stopped on the threshhold and looked up, where the ravens were flying.

'At them?' I asked.

'Yes, at them,' my mother answered.

Once again a shot rang out and tore through the ashes in the air, while the ravens croaked, invulnerable.

'They're laughing,' I observed.

'Are you still drunk?' my mother said.

I watched her; it was as if she were keeping an eye on me, I'm telling you.

'Was I drunk?' I asked.

'Don't you even know?' my mother said. 'You came back just like your father when he came back drunk. In a black mood. And you threw yourself on my bed, you made me sleep on the sofa.'

Another shot rang out.

'I don't understand what happens to you,' my mother continued. 'Your grandfather sang and joked when he drank.'

A fourth shot went up from a garden, a fifth followed, but the ravens flew through the high ash of the sky, always invulnerable, never changing course, croaking, laughing.

'Why so many ravens?' I exclaimed.

Now my mother was paying attention to the birds, watching, expecting one to fall.

'Are they really shooting at them?' I asked her.

A sixth, a seventh shot missed, and my mother lost her temper.

'It's useless. They're not hitting them,' she said.

She went back in the house and came back in a flash with a double-barrelled shotgun, and she, too, began to shoot.

Bang! Bang!

But nothing altered the irrational flight of the ravens.

'They're laughing,' I observed.

'Bang! Bang! Bang!' my mother responded.

Then the voice of a fat woman rose from the foot of the stairs, bringing news to my mother, shouting to her, between the shots and the ravens, 'Fortunate mother!'

XLV

Without a word, my mother went back into the kitchen and sat down.

There was the lit brazier in the middle, and she, little by little, gripped the firetongs in her hand, then moved them, dangled them, then stuck them into the ashes and turned the embers over little by little, then she got up and went to the stove and I was thinking she hadn't understood a thing.

'Will you eat with me before you go?' she asked me.

'Whatever you want,' I said. 'Whatever you want.'

I was thinking that she hadn't understood a thing, and I was even ready to do something for her, even though my journey in Sicily was already finished. Dear old woman; fortunate mother! She asked me if I would be happy with a herring, like the day before, or if I wanted a little chicory. She asked me if in the meantime I wanted a cup of coffee, and she gave herself over to preparing the coffee, and I watched her movements around the coffeepot and the oven, I saw her withdraw into her chores as every woman withdraws, and I feared for her solitude, for my own, for my father's, and for that of my brother, dead in the war.

'What time are you leaving?' she asked me.

Sicily had become motionless, and suffering from that, I told her I wanted to arrive in Siracusa in time to leave that evening. She ground the coffee, and while grinding she calculated the time necessary to catch the trains and bus. Then she said, 'I hope you're not going to enlist, at least.'

Then I knew she had understood everything. 'Oh!' I exclaimed.

And she added: 'You'll come back some other time.'

'Are you glad I came to see you?' I asked.

And she said: 'Of course. It's good to talk with a son, after fifteen years . . .'

She finished grinding and a rustle of water overflowing on the fire drew her again to the stove, to all those objects of her solitude. She continued: 'The years come and go, sons come and go . . .'

And while the crows shouted outside the window, she said: 'These crows!'

'But what attracted them here?' I said.

My mother shrugged her shoulders. 'Every now and then they show up.'

In the silence that followed I asked her: 'Who was it?'

My mother looked at the things of our childhood scattered around the kitchen, she looked far off, then nearer, nearer; she said: 'It was Liborio.'

'The third one of us,' I said.

And she: 'He hadn't yet been out in the world and he was happy when they called him up. He sent me postcards from places he saw. Three last year, two this year. Beautiful cities! He must have liked them.'

'The cities where the war is being fought?' I asked.

'I believe so,' she answered.

'And he was happy?' I cried.

I really shouted it out, then I added: 'A pretty idea, for the boy!'

My mother said: 'Don't think badly of him now.'

'Badly?' I cried. 'What are you thinking? He must have been a hero.'

My mother looked at me as if I were talking bitterly. 'No!' she said. 'He was a poor boy. He wanted to see the world. He loved the world.'

'Why are you looking at me that way?' I cried. 'He was brave. He conquered. He won.'

More loudly I cried: 'And he died for us. For me, for you, for all Sicilians, to allow all these things to continue, this Sicily, this world . . . He loved the world!'

'No!' my mother said. 'No! He was a boy, you were boys together. You were eleven when he was seven. You . . .'

'Give me that coffee,' I cried.

'Okay,' my mother responded.

And she filled a cup and brought it to me. Putting it on the table in front of me, she added: 'I imagine I wouldn't have seen him again anyway. Poor boy! He loved the world.'

XLVI

I saw her withdraw into her thoughts of the poor boy who loved the world, and saw her brood over the desire of every boy to know the world, to walk through beautiful cities, to meet women. While I drank my coffee, my mother looked at me as if I had a very strange look on my face; as if, for example, I were drinking my coffee in dismay and in anger. Really, I think I was reacting to the thought in her of a poor boy, and the idea in me of a seven-year-old. I didn't want a soldier to be seven years old. So I cried out, with real dismay or real anger: 'The devil!'

My mother sat down again in the chair in front of the brazier, and asked, very softly: 'There's only one thing I don't understand. Why did that woman call me fortunate?'

Right away I said: 'But that's clear. Because his death honours you.'

And she: 'His death honours me?'

And I: 'Dying, he brought honour to himself . . .'

Again she looked at me as if I were talking out of bitterness. In fact, there was a steadiness in the look she had cast over me as soon as I appeared: a suspicion, a reproach. Reproachfully she asked: 'And that's why I'm fortunate?'

I said, stubbornly: 'The honour reflects back on you. You gave birth to him.'

And she, still reproachfully: 'But I've lost him now. I should call myself unfortunate.'

And I: 'Not at all. Losing him you've gained him. You are fortunate.'

Speechless, my mother thought for a moment. Still she looked at me with suspicion, with reproach. And she seemed to feel that she was at my mercy. She asked me: 'Are you sure that woman wasn't playing a joke on me?'

'Oh, no!' I responded. 'She knew what she was saying.'

'She really thought I was fortunate?' she said.

'Oh, yes,' I answered. 'She would have liked to be in your place.'

And she: 'In my place? Like me?'

And I: 'Like you with Liborio dead . . . She would have been proud.'

She: 'So she envied me.'

I: 'All the women envy you.'

But still my mother looked at me with suspicion. She felt that she was at my mercy, that was clear. And now she burst out: 'But what are you saying?'

'I'm telling the truth,' I said. 'It's even written in books. Don't you remember anything from your schoolbooks?'

She: 'I only went up to third year.'

And I: 'You must have studied a little history.'

She: 'Mazzini and Garibaldi!'

I: 'And Caesar, Mucius Scaevola, Cincinnatus, Coriolanus. Don't you remember anything about the history of Rome?'

She: 'I remember what Cornelia, the mother of the Gracchi, said.'

I: 'Good! What did Cornelia say?'

She: 'She said that her children were her jewels.'

I: 'See? Cornelia was proud of her children.'

Now my mother smiled. 'How silly!' she exclaimed. 'But Cornelia's children weren't dead.'

'Exactly!' I said. 'They weren't dead yet. But why do you think Cornelia was proud of them?'

'Why?'

And I said: 'Because she knew they were ready to die. Cornelia was a Roman mother.'

My mother shrugged, speechless once again, and continued to look at me with suspicion.

'You see?' I continued. 'That woman considered you a sort of Cornelia. Doesn't it please you to be a sort of Cornelia?'

'I don't know,' my mother responded, suspiciously.

She asked: 'What was this Cornelia like?'

'Oh, she was a great woman!' I said. 'A noblewoman, a matron . . .'

And my mother: 'A beautiful woman?'

And I: 'Beautiful and wise. Tall. Blonde. Like you, I think.'

'So there you go!' my mother exclaimed. 'But why did they write about her in the books?'

'All by virtue of her children,' I cried.

'A fortunate woman!' my mother exclaimed.

And I cried: 'See? Just as you, too, are fortunate . . .'

My mother gave a start: 'I?' She was red in the face, afire and aflame with her shawl round her shoulders, as she exclaimed in a rush: 'Are you trying to say they'll also write about me in books?'

'More or less,' I said. 'About you and your son. You already belong to the books.'

My mother was deeply upset. She could no longer restrain herself, and she was no longer suspicious. 'Belong to the books? To the books?' she shouted.

'To history,' I said. 'Didn't you know? He's left the world and entered history. And you with him.'

'Me with him?' shouted my mother, deeply upset.

'You with him. You with him,' I shouted.

'Do you think you still belong to this world?' I shouted. 'To this land here? To Sicily?'

Louder, I shouted: 'No, my dear. You'll see, they'll call on you and give you a medal.'

'A medal?' my mother shouted.

'Yes, they'll pin it to your chest,' I shouted.

And here I finally lowered my voice and continued more calmly: 'For what he has done for the world. For this city. For Sicily.'

I concluded: 'A medal for his service.'

But my mother, right at this moment, began to fall apart. 'How can it be?' she said. 'He was only a poor boy.'

And I began to be afraid. I also began to remember.

XLVII

What did it mean to be a poor boy?

I looked around me at the kitchen, at the stove and the clay pot on it, and beyond it the kneading board for the bread, and then the container for water, the sink, the chairs, the table, the old clock said to be my grandfather's on the wall; and, looking, I was afraid. Afraid, I also looked at my mother. Wrapped in her shawl, among her things, she was like any one of them; full of time, of past humanity, of childhood and what follows, men and sons, all outside history. Here inside she would continue her life, and she would keep roasting her herring on the brazier, she would keep wearing my father's shoes on her feet. I looked at her and I was afraid.

And I asked myself who was more of a poor boy.

Who was more of a poor boy?

I was afraid, I repeat. And at the same time I was beginning to remember. As I began to remember I took out a cigarette and lit it. It was my first cigarette that day, and my only one, the same one left over from my drunken night. I lit it, threw away the match, and, remembering which cigarette it was, I found myself little by little with tears on my hands as I smoked.

Still smoking, I went outside. Caw, caw, caw, shouted the ravens flying through the ashen sky. I went down into the street, went along the street of that Sicily which was no longer a journey, but motionless, and I smoked and cried.

'Ah! Ah! He's crying! Why is he crying?' shouted the crows among themselves, following me.

I continued my walk without answering, and an old black woman followed me, too. 'Why are you crying?' she asked.

I didn't respond, and I went on, smoking, crying; and a tough guy who was waiting on the piazza with his hands in his pockets asked me, too: 'Why are you crying?'

He, too, followed me, and still crying, I passed in front of a church. The priest saw us, me and those following me, and asked the old woman, the tough guy, the crows: 'Why is this man crying?'

He joined us, and some street urchins saw us and exclaimed:

'Look! He's smoking and crying!'

They also said: 'He's crying because of the smoke!' And they followed me with the others, bringing their game along, too.

In the same way a barber followed me and a carpenter, a man in rags, a girl with her head wrapped in a scarf, a second man in rags. They saw me and they asked: 'Why are you crying?' Or they asked those who were already following me: 'Why is he crying?' And they all became my followers: a cart driver, a dog, men of Sicily, women of Sicily, and finally a Chinaman. 'Why are you crying?' they asked.

But I had no response to give them. I wasn't crying for any reason. Deep down I wasn't even crying; I was remembering; and in the eyes of others my remembering looked like crying.

What could I do? I continued along my street. And I came to the feet of a naked woman of bronze who was dedicated to the fallen soldiers, and I found around it all my friends of the day before, the Sicilians I had met and with whom I had spoken during my journey.

'There are other duties,' the Big Lombard told me. 'Don't cry.'

'Don't cry,' my sick friends said to me.

'Don't cry,' my women friends said to me.

And my little friend with the oranges, even he said to me, 'Don't cry.'

The man from Catania was there, and said: 'He's right. Don't cry.'

'Heh!' said the little old man with the voice of a dry twig.

'But I'm not crying for you,' I said. 'I'm not crying.'

I sat down on the step at the foot of the bronze woman, and the friends circled round me, they thought I was crying for them. 'I'm not crying,' I continued. And I cried. 'I'm not crying. I'm getting over being drunk.'

'What does he mean?' said Whiskers to Without Whiskers.

'He's hiding something,' said Without Whiskers to Whiskers.

'I'm not crying,' I continued. 'I'm not hiding anything.'

And the man Ezechiele cried out: 'The world is very wronged!'

'But I'm not crying in this world,' I replied.

The widow said: 'He's crying for his mother.'

The other woman said: 'He's crying for his dead brother.'

'No, no,' I replied. 'I'm not crying inside. I'm not crying in this world.'

And I said again that in fact I wasn't crying at all, I wasn't crying for anyone, not for Sicily or for anything else, for nothing in the world, and I dismissed them, I asked them all to go away, I said again that I was getting over being drunk.

The knife grinder asked me: 'Oh, where did you get drunk?'

'In the cemetery,' I told him. 'But we don't need to talk about it.'

'Ah!' the knife grinder said.

And I was done smoking, I was done remembering. And I stopped crying.

XLVIII

Then I raised my eyes to the nude bronze woman of the monument.

She was a beautiful young woman in her twice-natural dimensions and her smooth bronze skin; my mother would have declared her shapely; she had legs, thighs, back, belly, arms, everything that makes a woman a woman, really as if created fresh from the rib of man. Her sex was also subtly drawn; and long hair fell round her neck with sexual grace; her face smiled with a sexual cunning, because of all the honey in her, and because she was standing there nude in the middle of things, twice as large as necessary, in bronze.

I got up and circled round her, to examine her better. I went behind her, round her sides and then behind her again. My friends observed me, and the old men winked at me, the women and girls looked at one another with their heads bowed, and the Big Lombard gravely cleared his throat.

'It's really a woman,' I said.

The knife grinder came closer, planted himself next to me on the pedestal and raised his eyes too. 'Of course,' he exclaimed. 'It's a woman.'

We circled round her together, with our eyes still raised. 'She's got milk there,' the knife grinder observed. And laughed.

The girls laughed from the foot of the monument. The Big Lombard smiled. 'It's a woman,' I said again. I took one or two steps back on the pedestal, and the knife grinder did the same, both of us looked at the woman in her totality.

'Not bad, eh?' the knife grinder asked.

I pointed her smile out to him. And the knife grinder elbowed me. 'Ha! Ha!' he said.

The woman stood straight, one arm raised towards the sky and the other folded across her chest, almost touching an armpit. She smiled. 'She knows everything,' the knife grinder said.

At the foot of the pedestal, a girl laughed and the knife grinder added: 'She knows everything there is to know.'

'She knows even more,' I said. 'She knows she's invulnerable.'

'Really?' my interlocutor exclaimed.

'It's clear,' I said. 'She knows that she's made of bronze.'

'Ah, there you go!' exclaimed my interlocutors.

And I continued, 'One can tell, no?'

'One can tell,' my interlocutors noted.

I went down a step and sat down again. Everyone took a few steps back, everyone sat down.

'This woman is for them,' I said.

Everyone agreed, and I added: 'They're not ordinary dead, they don't belong to the world, they belong to something else, and this woman is theirs.'

'Ahem!' the soldier had said.

'Isn't it nice on our part to dedicate a woman to them?' I continued. 'In this woman we celebrate them.'

'Ahem!' the soldier had said. 'Ahem! Ahem!'

'And in this woman,' I continued, 'in this woman . . .'

The soldier interrupted me by speaking inside me, saying loudly: 'Ahem!'

'Ahem?' my interlocutors asked, sitting around me.

'Nothing,' I said. 'I only said, "Ahem!"'

But again the soldier spoke inside me, and again he said: 'Ahem!'

'What's all this about?' Whiskers and Without Whiskers asked each other.

'It's a code word,' I answered.

The Sicilians looked at each other.

'Ah!' said the man Porfirio.

'Of course,' said the man Ezechiele.

'Of course,' said the knife grinder.

And the Big Lombard agreed with a nod. Everyone agreed. Someone said: 'Even I know it.'

'What?' Whiskers asked.
'What?' asked Without Whiskers.
Up above, over all this, the woman of bronze smiled.
'And is it a lot to suffer?' asked the Sicilians.

Epilogue

XLIX

These were my conversations in Sicily, over three days and their respective nights. They finished as they had begun. But I must note that something else happened after they ended.

I went back to my mother's to take my leave, and I found her in the kitchen washing a man's feet.

The man was sitting with his back to the door and he was very old: she, kneeling on the floor, was washing his old feet in a basin. 'I'm leaving, Mamma,' I told her. 'It's time for the bus.'

At the other side of the man my mother raised her head. 'You're not eating with us, then?' she responded.

The man did not turn round, either at my words or at hers. He had white hair, he was very old, and he hung his head. He seemed profoundly absorbed, or asleep. 'Is he sleeping?' I whispered to my mother.

'No. He's crying, the fool,' she answered.

And added: 'It's always been that way. He cried when I gave birth and he's crying now, too.'

I whispered: 'What? That's Papa?'

He, meanwhile, paid us no attention.

I went closer to look him in the face and saw he was hiding it in his hands. He seemed to me, in any case, too old; for a moment I almost thought he was my grandfather. I also thought he might be my mother's vagrant. 'He's just come back?' I asked, whispering.

My mother shook her head disapprovingly.

'He's crying,' she said. 'He doesn't know that I'm fortunate.'

Here she left the man's old feet alone in the water of the basin, and got up to pull me aside. 'By the way, you got me confused with that Cornelia,' she said. 'It wasn't on the battlefield that her sons, her Gracchi, died.'

'It wasn't on the battlefield? I exclaimed, still whispering.

'No,' my mother continued. 'I looked it up in your children's books, when you were out.'

'Okay,' I said. And I kissed her on the forehead. 'Bye.'

'Don't you want to say hello to him?' my mother asked.

I hesitated, looking at the old man, then I said: 'I'll say hello to him another time. Let him be.' And I left the house, on tiptoe.

Afterword

(This piece was first published as a foreword to the first English translation.)

Elio Vittorini is one of the very best of the new Italian writers. He was born on 23 July, 1908, in Syracuse in Sicily and spent his boyhood in various parts of Sicily where his father was a stationmaster on the railways of that island. He is not a regional writer, for Italy is certainly not a region, and Vittorini from the time he was old enough to leave home without permission at seventeen learned his Italy in the same way American boys who ran away from home learned their own country.

The Italy that he learned and the America that the American boys learned has little to do with the Academic Italy or America that periodically attacks all writing like a dust storm and is always, until everything shall be completely dry, dispersed by rain.

Rain to an academician is probably, after the first fall has cleared the air, H_2O with, of course, traces of other things. To a good writer, needing something to bring the dry country alive so that it will not be a desert where only

such cactus as New York literary reviews grow dry and
sad, inexistent without the watering of their benefactors,
feeding on the dried manure of schism and the dusty taste
of disputed dialectics, their only flowering a desiccated
criticism as alive as stuffed birds, and their steady mulch
the dehydrated cuds of fellow critics; such a writer finds
rain to be made of knowledge, experience, wine, bread,
oil, salt, vinegar, bed, early mornings, nights, days, the
sea, men, women, dogs, beloved motor cars, bicycles,
hills and valleys, the appearance and disappearance of
trains on straight and curved tracks, love, honor and dis-
obey, music, chamber music and chamber pots, negative
and positive Wassermanns, the arrival and non-arrival of
expected munitions and/or reinforcements, replacements
or your brother. All these are a part of rain to a good
writer along with your hated or beloved mother, may she
rest in peace or in pieces, porcupine quills, cock grouse
drumming on a bass-wood log, the smell of sweet-grass
and fresh smoked leather and Sicily.

In this book the rain you get is Sicily. I care nothing
about the political aspects of the book (they were many
at the time) nor about Vittorini's politics (I have examined them carefully and to me they are honorable). But
I care very much about his ability to bring rain with
him when he comes if the earth is dry and that is what
you need.

He has more books about the north of Italy that he
knows and loves and about other parts of Italy. This is
a good one to start with.

If there is any rhetoric or fancy writing that puts you off at the beginning or the end, just ram through it. Remember he wrote the book in 1937 under Fascism and he had to wrap it in a fancy package. It is necessarily wrapped in cellophane to pass the censor. But there is excellent food once you unwrap it.

Ernest Hemingway
Cortina D'Ampezzo, 1949

About the Author
and Translator

ELIO VITTORINI was born in Siracusa, Sicily, in 1908. An acclaimed translator (Defoe, Faulkner, Lawrence, Steinbeck and Somerset Maugham), broadcaster and activist all his life, it was not until 1941 that *Conversations in Sicily* first appeared. A highly outspoken critic of Mussolini and his fascist government, Vittorini was arrested and jailed in 1942. He died in 1996.

ALANE MASON is a senior editor at W.W. Norton who, just as Vittorini learned to read English by translating *Robinson Crusoe*, learned to read Italian by translating *Conversations in Sicily*. Although she was born in America, her family come from Sicily, where she spends ever-increasing amounts of time. She lives in New York.

THE FASTEST SELLING LINE OF
SPORTS CAR BOOKS EVER PUBLISHED

A series of low-cost books designed to meet the skyrocketing demand for more information on these trim, sleek, high-performance machines. Each volume, written by an expert, deals with one of the more popular makes or with some general phase of the sport. Fully illustrated, these attractive and practical manuals are designed for the thousands of owners, would-be owners, and enthusiastic devotees of rallies, races, and expert road driving.

SPORTS CAR PRESS
Publishers of Automobile and Aircraft Books
Distributed by CROWN PUBLISHERS
419 Park Avenue South, New York, N.Y. 10016